A Little Bit Dead

A Little Bit Dead

◆ ◆ ◆ ◆ ◆

Chap Reaver

Delacorte
Press

Published by
Delacorte Press
Bantam Doubleday Dell Publishing Group, Inc.
666 Fifth Avenue
New York, New York 10103

Library of Congress Cataloging in Publication Data

Reaver, Chap.
    A little bit dead / Chap Reaver.
        p.   cm.
    Summary: In 1876, after interfering with the attempted lynching of a young Yahi Indian named Shanti, eighteen-year-old Reece finds his own life in danger and becomes intimately involved in the future of Shanti's people.
    ISBN 0-385-30801-9
    1. Yahi Indians—Juvenile fiction. [1. Yahi Indians—Fiction. 2. Indians of North America—Fiction.   3. West (U.S.)—Fiction.] I. Title.
    PZ7.R23765Li   1992
    [Fic]—dc20   92-7185   CIP   AC

October 1992

Manufactured in the United States of America

10 9 8 7 6 5 4 3 2 1

BVG

Once again for Dixie;
and for Chappie and Scott

◆ 1 ◆

March 1876

Packy snorted softly and tossed her head the way she does when she smells trouble. I figured she had caught scent of a mountain lion or grizzly, so I dropped out of the saddle and carried my Winchester up to the crest of the rise. I took my hat off and crawled the last few feet.

The Indian kid was naked except for ankle-high moccasins and he was bloody from his chest on down. He stood with his head lowered, like he was ashamed of being tied up.

The three lynchers had their backs to me, and the short one was trying to throw the hanging rope over a side branch. A stick was tied to the end, and when he threw it up toward the branch the other two cheered, then ducked and hollered when the stick came whirling back down. There was a lot of loud talk and whooping it up. The short guy scuffled around with the fat guy to see who would try it next.

I scooted to my left a few inches and their prisoner jerked his head up and looked square at me. Our eyes held for a second from fifty, sixty yards, then he dropped his head back down.

I was pulling a winter's load of furs on a travois, taking advantage of the early break in the weather. It had been a hard winter, and I needed supplies and some company. For five months the only voice I had heard was my own. This looked like the kind of trouble it was best to ride on around.

I started to scoot backward, and the Indian looked up at me again. He didn't beg, he just locked his eyes to mine and left it up to me. I wished he hadn't of done that.

The fat guy took a try with the rope and succeeded in knocking his hat off and falling over backward. The other two slapped their legs and pointed. I sighted my rifle for fifty steps, took a deep breath in, a half breath out, a full bead, and shot his hat. It tumbled and sailed off a few feet. The lynchers quick sobered and looked up.

I put my hat on to show myself and hollered down, "Unbuckle your gun belts and let 'em fall."

The short guy said, "What for?"

" 'Cause I got a rifle."

They looked at each other, and the fat guy nodded. They dropped their gun belts, and I got up and walked down the slope. I didn't recognize the short guy or the fat guy, but I remembered seeing the other man in town last summer. He was a mean-looking character with a little tiny flap where his left ear used to be. The right ear was a regular.

I said, "What's going on?"

Shorty said, "We're fixin' to hang us a Injun."

"What for?"

Shorty smiled a tobacco smile. " 'Cause he's a Injun's what for. Come on and have a drink."

The fat guy said, "It's all legal, sonny. We got papers."

I looked over at the young brave. The blood on his chest was from whip cuts. He had taken some lashes on his legs and arms, and I wondered what his back looked like. I said, "What'd you whip him so much for?"

Shorty said, " 'Cause, he's a Injun." He smiled his brown smile again and looked to his two pals for support.

I said, "Back off and sit down."

Ear said, "What do you plan to do, kid?"

"I don't know yet. Sit down."

They all three sat down, and I gathered up the gun belts and backed away. The Indian hadn't moved. I motioned for him to come over by me. He had to hop, and I could tell that he hated that, looking so foolish and helpless. I pointed to the ground, and he sat down. His back looked even worse than his chest.

I got down cross-legged facing the three lynch men. "Well, here we are," I said. It felt good to be talking to somebody, even these guys. I lifted a Colt from the holster and began to pull shells, dropping them into my shirt pocket. "You fellows have any interesting stories to tell?"

The three of them looked back at me silently. I said, "Anything real funny ever happen to you?"

That didn't start anything either. Packy had walked up behind me dragging the travois. I said, "I'll tell you something that happened to me one time. It's pretty funny 'cause . . ."

The fat guy said, "You're meddlin' in serious government business, don't you know?" He pulled his jacket to the side to show me a badge pinned to his shirt. "Now you hand them guns back over, and we'll forget this happened."

"You don't want to hear my story, huh?"

He shook his head.

I said, "It's got a real good ending."

He nodded his head toward Packy. "Looks to me you'd want to tend to them furs instead of crowdin' in on us. Those are good-looking hides."

"Had a good winter." I started ejecting shells from the second gun. "I'm taking them into town. What do you say we all do this? We all go together and turn your prisoner in to the sheriff if he's done something worth hanging? Then we'll have that drink together, and I'll tell you my story. Maybe you fellows know some good saloon jokes."

Shorty said, "Why don't you just butt out and let us take care of a Injun?"

I said, "Are you the one did the whipping?"

Shorty turned his head to spit. "You some kind of Injun lover? That what you are, Injun lover?"

"No, but lynching is . . . What I mean is that you guys seemed to be getting so much pleasure out of it. Doesn't seem like proper behavior. Whipping a tied-up man don't strike me as manly neither."

Ear said, "You ever see what Injuns do to their prisoners?"

"I've heard the stories."

"Them stories is true," Shorty said. "They do a lot worse than just whippin'." He jerked his thumb at the boy. "I call that payback."

I looked at the whip cuts. "Calling it payback don't make it right."

I emptied the last gun and returned it to the holster. "Come on, let's ride to Macland."

Ear said, "We ain't got enough horses."

"Somebody walks we do," I said. "How about you, Shorty? The Indian kid can ride your horse. If you get tired, he can help you along a little with the whip. Call it payback if you want to."

Ear said, "I ain't riding into town with you, kid."

Fat man said, "Me neither."

Shorty grinned again. "I'm stayin' right here." He leaned back on his elbows.

We sat there and looked at each other. I needed to say something hard sounding. "What happened to your ear?"

"I ate it."

"Why?"

"What do you care?"

"I don't know. It must be something you get asked a lot though, huh?"

He turned and looked off. It seemed to me that he should have made up some kind of good answer about his missing ear. People are bound to notice a thing like that and be curious and make comments.

I said, "All right," pulled my knife and stood up. "Let's all just ride away from it, forget it happened." I cut the ropes from the brave's wrists. He kept his eyes on me as he worked with the knots at his ankles. When he got them free, I made washing motions with my hands and pointed to the creek. He said some words I didn't understand, then turned and trotted to the stream.

When I turned the fat man was looking at my face. I said, "I can't figure out how to do this."

He laughed. "Worked yourself into a fix now, ain't you, boy?"

The kid was lying awash in the creek. There was still some snow along the banks, and I wondered how he could stand the icy water. I slung the three gun belts over my shoulder. "You follow our tracks. I'll drop your sidearms along the trail and tie your horses up before dark."

"Leave us one horse," the fat man said. "We can trade off, two walking, one riding. Still be slow going."

"Leave a gun too," Ear said. "You know, snakes or something."

I said, "Why don't you let your hair go long on that side?"

Ear gave me a look that would melt a cannon.

I said, "I guess long on both sides would be better. If you just let one side grow long, people might think you're covering up something. Like maybe you don't have one of your ears or something."

Ear kept looking at me with his teeth clamped together.

I said, "That fellow looks pretty good with his hair long that way." I looked at him washing off in the creek. "He could have both ears off and you'd never know it."

Shorty spit. "Injun lover."

I smiled. "That's me."

Packy followed me down to the stream where the three horses were tied. The brave looked better after his wash, but some of the lash cuts still oozed blood. I opened one of the bedrolls and tossed him a shirt. It must have been the fat man's shirt, from the size. He was shivering as he fumbled around with the buttons, but finally got it done.

No pants. The three men hadn't moved, so I laid the rifle down and used my knife to start a cut in the blanket, then ripped off a strip about three feet wide. He watched me closely. I wrapped the strip around my waist, like a woman's skirt. He got the idea and grunted a word, something like "Hakka."

When he got the skirt on, he seemed to stand taller, like he felt better with his privates covered. I motioned him up on a horse, and he swung up in one easy movement without using the stirrup. We rode off, climbing a little rise side by side, trailing the two other horses.

At the top of the rise I hip-turned in the saddle and looked back at the three lynchers. They were standing by the tree, hands in back pockets. Shorty spit. I thought about waving to them but figured it wouldn't help. We were never going to be friends anyway. The best I could hope for was that I wouldn't see them again.

2

Most of the Indians I had seen around were string beans, but this one was barrel-chested with well-formed muscles. He had a broad forehead, deep-set eyes, a wide mouth, and a squared-off jaw. I figured him for about my age, seventeen or eighteen, but he could have been younger.

I wished we could talk. I liked solitude, but five months of it was enough. It would be a pleasure to ride a long trail on a good horse and get to know a stranger with slow conversation, letting the talk and the horses find their natural pace.

I pointed to myself and said, "Reece." The kid looked at me. I said it again, "Reece," tapping my chest. I pointed to him and raised my eyebrows.

After half a mile he said, "Leece." We rode another few minutes before he turned in the saddle, put his palm against his chest, and said, "Shanti Ma Teck."

I said, "Shanti." He said, "Leece," and we smiled and nodded. For the next mile we rode along saying, "Shanti" and "Leece" back and forth to each other. It was better than no talk at all and had a good feel to it.

We came to a lone cottonwood tree, and I dropped

off Packy and uncinched the saddles from the two lynchers' horses. Shanti swung off his horse and removed the
saddle. He pointed to the saddlebags, then to himself
and looked at me. I shrugged my shoulders, and Shanti
took a pouch from the saddlebag. He untied the thong
and poured out four arrowheads and a piece of folded
paper. He said, "Tapayan," or something like that.

Shanti returned the arrowheads and paper to his
pouch and tied it. He tucked the pouch under his rope
belt, then stared down at his feet and legs.

I laid the gun belts across a saddle and dropped the
bullets on the ground. They wouldn't like it, having to
carry their saddles the rest of the way. Shanti said,
"Leece." When I looked up, he fingered his blanket skirt
then put his hands under the shirt and pushed out with
his fists like he had large breasts. He walked around,
swaying his hips and talking in a high-pitched voice. I
laughed pretty hard at his joke, and he laughed along
with me.

We mounted back up, Shanti bareback now, and
rode southwest. It was different now that we had
swapped names and shared a laugh. I decided to tell him
about myself.

"My name is Herbert Reece," I began. "I don't care
much for the first part, so I just go by Reece."

Shanti said, "Leece."

"Yeah. Me and my dad, we came out here three years
ago from back east. Kentucky, right across the river from
a place called Cincinnati. My mom and little sister are
still there. We were going to send for them when we'd
saved up enough money to buy some land."

I looked over at Shanti, and he turned to look back at
me. Our horses were at a nice, easy walk. "So, anyway it
went pretty good for a while, Shanti. We trapped in the

winter and scratched around, panning gold in the summer. We sent money back home and figured another year we could all be together. But then Dad died. He fell through the ice crossing the creek. He was in there too long, and I got him out, but he died anyway. Real sick for a week, then one night he just passed away in his sleep."

When Shanti looked over, he had a sorrowful look. I guess he could tell by the sound of my voice.

"So I'm trapping by myself now, still panning some gold and saving money. Maybe next year I can send for Mom and Sis."

We went down a small hillside and passed a huge old pine tree. Shanti leaned over and gave the trunk a pat as he passed. I rode by the tree, too, but I didn't mess around with it.

We rode side by side, and Shanti began talking. He used words that I didn't understand, made of lot of gestures and grunts and click sounds, pointed here and there and made faces. Some happy faces, angry faces, and some sad faces. I made faces back at him and tried to nod and smile at the right times as he told me his stories and interesting experiences.

We came to a creek and let the horses drink. Macland was only a few miles away, and the wagon road into the town was just over the next rise. Shanti drank from the stream, lying on his belly. He took a long pull, then looked around before lowering his head again, the way deer do it.

I tied the reins to some limber branches of a streamside sapling. I smiled at the thought of Shorty, Ear, and Fat Man walking all the miles we had put between us. They didn't strike me as good walkers.

I knelt beside Shanti and sluiced up a few handfuls of

the cold creek water, then took the kerchief from around my neck and soaked it in the stream. Shanti watched me wipe my face and neck. I rinsed the kerchief, wrung it out, and handed it to him. Shanti used it and washed it out before giving it back.

I tapped my chest and pointed toward town, then pointed at Shanti and made a shooing motion with both hands. He nodded. I offered my hand for a farewell shake, and Shanti looked at it, then frowned at me. I reached down and caught his right wrist, and we shook hands. He liked it, and I did too.

I turned away and put a foot in the stirrup. Shanti said, "Leece." He was bent over untying the rawhide strip that held his ankle-high moccasin on his left foot. He fished an arrowhead from his pouch and knotted the strip together at the ends. He made a loop and fitted it around the neck of the arrowhead, then pulled it tight. He approached me and put the rawhide necklace over my head. The arrowhead hung at my chest. Shanti gave it a pat, looked me flat in the eye, and grunted.

I took off my neckerchief and handed it to him. Shanti made a headband out of it, and it looked good on him. We admired our gifts and touched them and grinned.

I mounted up, touched the arrowhead, and said, "Shanti." He patted his head and said, "Leece." I nudged Packy with my heels, and she lunged across the creek and began climbing the rise. At the top I turned in the saddle. Shanti was standing by the creek. I raised a hand, and he raised his. He was a pretty good guy to ride with.

⟐ 3 ⟐

Packy and I got into Macland just before sundown, and I hitched up in front of the trading post. The temperature had dropped below freezing, and the wind was gusting from the northwest, promising weather. Sometimes those late-winter storms are the worst.

Mr. Fitsimmons was behind the counter telling yarns to a couple hangers-on who sat beside an old wood stove. He glanced up at me and raised a hand while he went on with his story.

"So Saint Peter asks the first guy, 'How many times were you unfaithful to your wife?' and the ole boy says, 'Just twicet.' So Saint Pete gives him this little donkey to ride around heaven."

Fitsimmons let fly a tobacco spit that looped over the counter, hung in the air, and dropped onto the side of the wood stove. *Hissss.* His two cronies followed this example.

"Saint Pete asks the second guy, and he says, 'Just oncet,' and Saint Pete gives him this here pony."

Hisss . . . hissss, hissss.

"The third guy, when Saint Pete asks him says, 'I

was never unfaithful to my wife,' and so ole Saint Pete gives him this fine stallion with a show saddle on it.

"Well, a few days go by and the first two guys come up on the ole boy on his stallion and he's cryin' and taking on. They asks him what's the matter and the ole boy wipes his eyes. 'I just saw my wife,' he says. 'And she was aridin' a prairie dog.' "

There was a lot of knee slapping, shoulder punching, and hee-hawing. After it quieted down, Fitsimmons said, "She was riding a prairie dog," and they all went to slapping themselves again.

After it finally settled down again, one of the loafers said, "Ridin' a prairie dog," and got a few more chuckles, but you could tell they had about milked it dry.

Fitsimmons said, "What brings you to town, Reece?"

"I brought in some furs."

"Let's go see 'em." He picked up his revolver from the counter, a short-barreled Navy Colt, and dropped it in his pocket, butt first, with the barrel sticking up. He came out from behind the counter and waved his two cronies on ahead of him. Fitsimmons wasn't the trusting kind, but he was a fair and honest trader. He and my dad had been good friends.

He ran his hand over the furs and lifted up a few pelts. "You want to be paid in coin?"

I shook my head. "Your check will be fine. Maybe ten dollars' cash, and I'll be needing some supplies."

Fitsimmons nodded. He told his two pals to unload the furs in his storage barn around back. "You be staying at the hotel, Reece?"

"Yep, for the night."

"Ten dollars be enough? Lizzie's brought in a new

whore." He spit in the dust. "Might put some hair on your chest."

I laughed along with the other two. "What's she like?"

"Little bitty thing," Fitsimmons said. He held his hand, palm down across his shirt pockets. "Dress out about eighty, ninety pounds. She fell off the roof, you couldn't catch her."

The two loafers were listening closely. One of them said, "Them little ones," shaking his head back and forth and grinning.

I said, "Ten dollars will be enough. Leave the travois out back, and if you'll stable my horse, we'll settle up in the morning."

The loafer said, "You gonna try the little whore?"

"No."

His face saddened, and he shook his head as he led Packy away.

I bought a pair of Levi Strauss pants, a wool shirt, socks, and a neckerchief, a blue one like the one I had given Shanti. Mr. Fitsimmons added everything up on a slip of paper and handed it to me along with ten silver dollars. Big sides of bacon were hanging from the ceiling. Mr. Fitsimmons saw me looking at them. "Been smoked eight days with hickory," he said.

I said, "You know a guy with one ear?"

"Yeah, that'd be Colby." He worked up a spit and tilted his head back.

I stepped to the side. "You know much about him?"

Fitsimmons folded his arms across his chest. "I know he used to be cavalry. Last I heard he was some kind of ranger or marshal or some such. Supposed to exterminate Indians, all the ones that didn't get back to the reservation. They call them 'hostiles' now. How do you know him, Reece?"

"Ran into him half a day's ride from here. He and two others were about to hang an Indian boy." I told him the whole story and described the short guy and the older fat guy.

He closed his eyes and shook his head. "Can't place those other two. I'll ask around, Reece. You come by the saloon later and I'll buy you a drink, maybe play some cards and take some of that ten dollars off you."

I went out the back door to get my rifle and saddle-bags. It had dropped a few more degrees, and the wind made me lean against it. Winter was going to uncork one more storm before it turned loose. The two guys were stacking my furs in Fitsimmons's shed. As I approached, I heard one of them say, "The guy got the big horse 'cause he didn't cheat on his wife."

"Yeah."

"And the other guys, they got smaller horses 'cause they messed around a couple times."

"Uh-huh."

"And the guy with the stallion, he saw his ol' wife riding a prairie dog, see?"

"You couldn't ride a prairie dog, too small."

"I know, but it's just a joke, see? What the funny part is, the reason it's funny is that you get a smaller horse the more you mess around. And so this guy, he's being faithful to his wife and he thinks she's faithful too and he sees her and she's riding a prairie dog. Get it?"

I watched the other one think it over. "Do they bark, them prairie dogs?"

I flipped the saddlebags over my shoulder. It was full dark as I laughed my way over to the hotel, and a few flakes of snow were falling.

◆ 4 ◆

I felt good when I walked over to the saloon later wearing my new clothes over a fresh wash and shave. Fitsimmons and his two buddies were at a table toward the back. There were about fifteen men and some saloon girls around tables and at the bar. They all looked me over, and I wished I wasn't so fancy and hair-combed.

Fitsimmons looked up from his cards, pointed me to a chair, and twisted to wave over a girl from the bar. He said, "What are you drinking, Reece?"

"I'd like to try a beer."

The girl was small and slender with long brown hair. She wasn't all painted up like the others. Fitsimmons said, "Kathryn, this here's the fellow I was telling you about. Nice young boy, been trapping all winter all by hisself with no company or nothing." He turned to me, "Reece, this here is Miss Kathryn."

I nodded to the girl, and she nodded back at me, then dropped her head down real shy. Fitsimmons told her to bring me a beer and sit with us.

I decided to play with five dollars. I got chips from Fitsimmons. His dumb buddy said, "Hear you had some trouble with Colby."

"Yeah, I did."

The other one said, "What tribe was that Injun from?"

"I don't know."

Fitsimmons said, "What was he wearing?"

"Nothing," I said. "Just moccasins is all."

The dumb guy said, "He have a feather in his hair?"

"No."

"His hair tied in those knots?"

"No, it just hung loose. I gave him my neckerchief, one like this one." I fingered my new bandanna. "And he tied it around his head to hold his hair."

Fitsimmons said, "How come you give him your neckerchief?"

"Because he gave me something first. He gave me an arrowhead."

"What for?"

"It was . . . I think it was a gift, sort of a present. I think he was trying to thank me for turning him loose from the three that were going to hang him."

The other guy said, "I wouldn't be taking no presents from Injuns, I was you."

The dumb guy said, "You think he was Sioux, or Yahi or what?"

"I don't know. What difference does it make?"

"Some of them is worse than others."

"This one was nice. Wasn't anything scary or mean about him at all."

"All Indians is mean."

"Well, not this one."

We cut for the deal. They were playing five-card-draw poker, jacks to open, two-bit limit. Dad and I used to play poker for hours at a time when we got weathered in. He taught me a lot about the game and said that you can get to know a man better by playing poker with him.

I won the deal, anted up, and shuffled. Kathryn set the beer down on the table and pulled a chair to sit next to me. She smelled pretty too.

Nobody could open. I had only drunk beer one other time, and it made me dizzy and stupid. I sipped slowly and pretended it was good while the other guy dealt the cards. When I glanced at the girl, she smiled at me. I probably would have smiled back if other guys weren't there.

Fitsimmons said, "Cards is cold tonight," and we all agreed with that. When the dumb guy opened, I drew to an inside straight. I missed the straight, and Kathryn poked me in the ribs with her little fingers.

I asked Mr. Fitsimmons, "How come you carry your gun that way, in your pocket that way with the barrel up?"

"Harder for someone to take it away from you that way."

I said, "Doesn't it take you a long time to pull it out?"

"I can get it out pretty fast."

The dumb guy dealt. Fitsimmons looked at his cards and opened for a dime. "If you got to run, it won't fall out your pocket. Running is smarter than shooting sometimes."

The dumb guy said, "You won't catch me running from nobody."

I called the opening dime and tried to draw to another inside straight, missed it again, and got another poke in the ribs from Kathryn. I said, "Maybe you should kick me, I try that again."

On the next hand the dumb guy beat my two pair with three eights and giggled about it.

A few hands later I tried for another inside straight, missed it, and folded. I said, "Aren't you going to kick me?"

Kathryn shook her head. "Kicking's not what I got in mind for you."

That started me thinking. I had never been with a woman, but it was something that occupied my mind on many an occasion. I settled down and tried to play smart and wondered how much it cost to go upstairs with that girl.

Fitsimmons said, "Couple days ago this ole boy come riding in on a mule and hitched up in front of my place. Them muley men is funny, you know. Think mules is the greatest thing they are. So he gets off, walks behind his mule, lifts up its tail, and gives it a big kiss, right on the ass."

Mr. Fitsimmons shook his head back and forth. "Damnedest thing I ever saw, so when he comes in, I asked him, I asked him how come he kissed his mule on the ass like that, and he says, 'That's 'cause I got chapped lips.'

"So I says, 'Will that cure chapped lips?' and he says, 'No, but it sure will keep you from licking 'em.' "

Everyone laughed. I wished that I could tell jokes the way Mr. Fitsimmons could, but I didn't think it was right for him to say *ass* like that in front of everyone with Kathryn there.

I opened with a pair of aces and drew three cards. The aces didn't improve, and I bet a nickel. Fitsimmons raised a quarter. I thought about it a moment, then folded.

Mr. Fitsimmons slid the chips into his pile and grinned. "That's one you'll wonder about, Reece."

"You're right."

"Never know if I had you beat or was bluffing."

The dumb guy said, "What'd you have, Fitz?"

Mr. Fitsimmons said, "Ain't telling."

I shuffled the cards. The dumb guy said, "The hand's over, you could tell us what you had."

"I'm not gonna, though. Got to pay you want to see my cards. Besides, even if I told you, I might be lying."

"Tell us anyway."

Mr. Fitsimmons shook his head.

I began dealing around. The dumb guy said, "How come you let him run you, Reece? How come you didn't call 'stead of folding?"

I picked up my cards. "I think it's like Mr. Fitsimmons said about running being smarter than shooting sometimes."

"You won't catch me folding," he said.

Mr. Fitsimmons said, "That's why you lose all the time."

I remembered Shanti's arrowhead necklace and touched it through my shirt. I called openers, kept two eights, and drew another eight and two sevens. I raised the dime bet, got raised back a dime, and kicked a quarter. The dumb guy stayed the whole time. My full house won, and I was back over five dollars.

Kathryn put her hand on my leg!

I folded twice, then opened with three nines and won. We dealt around three times before I won a small pot with two aces. She just let her hand rest on my thigh, and I acted like I didn't even notice it was there.

I had six dollars and twenty-five cents, so I put five dollars' worth of chips in my shirt pocket. Kathryn made a little rubbing motion on my leg, and my jeans felt awful tight up around the buttons. I wanted to squirm around in the chair, but I was afraid she'd move her hand if I did.

I said, "How's your wife, Mr. Fitsimmons?"

"Not so good," he said. "Arthuritis is getting worse. Cora pretty much stays upstairs all the time the last few months."

"Could I come up and see her tomorrow before I go?"

"That'd be nice, Reece. She asks about you. She'll say, 'How is Herbert doing?' "

The dumb guy said, "Herbert. That your name?"

"Yeah."

He giggled about that. Kathryn squeezed my leg.

I lost to a better full house and had to get a dollar out of my pocket. Three nines won for me, and then I had to fold four hands in a row. One was an inside straight, and Kathryn gave my leg a nice little pat when I folded. On the next hand I drew to an open-ended straight, touched Shanti's arrowhead, and hit it. The pot got me a whole dollar ahead.

Kathryn said, "Win another dollar, and we'll have a party."

There was a lot of power in those words. I opened with a pair of aces, lost, and folded three hands. Then I lost with two pair. I pulled a dollar out of my pocket. Kathryn said, "Take all the chips out of your pocket, Mr. Reece. When you get 'em, you bet 'em."

I won a good pot with a straight. "Don't put that money away," she said. I drew to a flush and hit. The pot put me up over four dollars. Kathryn said, "Well?"

"One more," I said. I touched Shanti's arrowhead again.

It was a full house, kings over eights. The dumb guy was busted. He said, "I quit."

I said, "Me too."

Kathryn said, "Well?"

"Yeah, I guess."

Mr. Fitsimmons cashed my chips and grinned real big.

I walked in kind of a half crouch as I followed Kathryn toward the stairs. Fitsimmons said something about it to his two buddies. I tried to straighten up as I climbed the stairs but just couldn't. The whole room was laughing by the time we got to the top.

There was a large bed, neatly made, a small sofa, and a chest of drawers made of red maple. Near the window was a wash table with pitcher and bowl. I could see the snow blowing sideways across the window.

Kathryn walked to the bed, turned to me, and crossed her arms. I didn't know what to do, so I hooked my thumbs in my side pockets and did a good job of looking things over. "This is a nice room."

She tilted her head to the side, "Is this your first time, Reece?"

"Heck no."

"Well, come over here, then."

I walked over, taking my good old time. She put her arms around my neck and stood on her tiptoes while she pulled my head down for a kiss. She tasted like apples. "This is the worst part," she said. She pulled the money from my shirt, took out two dollars, and returned the rest. She walked over to the chest and dropped the coins in the top drawer. "That's over with."

She came back to me and began unbuttoning my shirt. "So, you're a trapper, then."

"Uh-huh. Yes, ma'am." There was nothing for me to

do with my hands while she unbuttoned the shirt. I let them hang down there.

"I've never done that," she said. "If you took me trapping, it would be my first time."

"I'd show you how."

"I'll bet you would, Reece. I'll bet you'd show me real nice. You sit on the bed."

I sat down and she pulled off my right boot. I raised my left leg. She took hold of my boot and said, "If I lied to you and told you I'd been trapping before, you'd know pretty quick that I was lying, wouldn't you?"

"Yes, ma'am. I guess I could tell."

"Do my buttons." I stood up and fumbled with those tiny buttons on the back of her dress while my knees shook. She said, "Nothing to be ashamed of, doing something for the first time."

"No, ma'am."

"Everybody has a first time."

I did the last button. She turned around and pulled the dress from her shoulders letting it fall to the floor. I almost fell with it. Her skin was so white. There were two narrow strips that held her slip up.

She said, "Would you like me to show you?"

"Yes, ma'am. I sure would."

And she did show me. She laughed a lot, and it was real nice but too quick, so she showed me again and helped me not be in such a big rush. I guess I got the hang of it pretty good, because the next time wasn't like anybody showing anybody anything. It was just being together in a perfect way. She opened her eyes and smiled back at me several times and made sweet little sounds and said my name and I think she had as much fun as me, more maybe, and afterward I wondered why it was me that had to do the two-dollar part. I had never been called "Reecie" before.

We lay together for a while and it was starting to be real good, Kathryn pressed up against me like that and fooling with the hair in back of my ear. It would have been nice to stay exactly like that all night.

"You better get up, Reece."

I didn't want to turn her loose, so I acted like I didn't hear.

"Reece."

"Hmm?"

"Come on. Get your clothes on."

I shook my head and held her tighter.

She pushed against my chest with her little hands. "Now, come on, Reece." She was just the right size.

"Call me Reecie again."

"No. Now, come on." Her voice sounded serious, so I let go of her, and she sat up real quick with her back to me.

I said, "Thanks, Kathryn" and reached out to touch the back of her arm.

She pulled her arm away. "You get yourself dressed."

I got up and picked my long johns off the floor. "Why are you in such a hurry, Kathryn?"

She dropped her slip over her head. "I'm a working girl, Reece. And you want to go down and tell your friends all about it, don't you?"

I pulled on a sock. "No, I'd rather talk to you awhile."

"Talk to me? Just talk?"

"Yeah. I've never really talked with a girl. Just Packy."

"Who's Packy?"

"She's my horse."

"You talk to your horse?"

"Sure."

"Does it talk back to you?"

"Sometimes. I mean, she knows what I say."

"Uh-huh."

"She does, really."

"Just talk?"

"Yeah."

She looked up at me for a moment, then walked to the sofa and sat down. "You can sit here," she patted the seat.

I sat beside her with my hands folded so I wouldn't touch her. She looked real prim and proper for a girl just wearing a slip. I said, "You know, when I told you that . . . when I said that this wasn't my first time. Well, it really was my first time."

Kathryn said, "Well, I would never have guessed, Reece."

"It was, though."

Kathryn said, "You can put your arm around me if you want to."

✦ 5 ✦

Snow streaked across the window. Kathryn had her head on my shoulder. Her hair smelled real sweet. I said, "Where are you from, Kathryn?"

"Saint Louis. How about you?"

"Cincinnati. Near there."

She said, "What are you, Reece? About sixteen?"

"Eighteen," I said. "You're about sixteen, aren't you?"

She laughed. "No, I'm eighteen, but I'm about a hundred years older than you are."

I tried to figure that out, and it didn't do any good. "What do you mean, a hundred years older than me?"

"I just am. You don't stay young very long, being a whore."

I said, "Don't call yourself a . . . don't call yourself any bad names."

"Reece, I could call myself the queen of England and it wouldn't change it." She didn't move for a few minutes. She said, "What brought you out here?"

"My dad. He and I came out a few years ago. We were going to send for the family when we had enough money to buy a spread." I squeezed her closer, and she

let me. "But Dad, he died. He fell through the ice crossing the creek and . . . Well, I pulled him out and got
him back to the cabin, but he died."

"Are you all by yourself, then?"

"Uh-huh."

"Do you get lonely?"

"Yeah, sometimes."

"Me too." She slid her hand inside my BVDs and
pressed against my short ribs. Her touch was warm and
soft on my bare skin. Women are a lot softer than men.

I said, "How can you be lonely with all that goes on
around here all the time?"

She raised her head and I kissed her. She smiled at
me and said, "Wished I'd have met you a year ago,
Reece." She moved her hand and touched my arrowhead
necklace. "What's this?"

I told her about my run-in with Colby, Shorty, the
fat guy, and about Shanti. "I think this is good luck," I
said. "Everytime I touched it I got good cards. I got to
meet you too. This morning I didn't have any friends my
own age. Now I've got two."

We sat together for a long time. Dad had told me
that he didn't think people made friends. He said it was
more a matter of finding them.

"You know what Dad said one time?"

"What?"

"He said that people out here, when they come out
here, they get more like they already are."

"What's that mean?"

"It means, suppose a guy is kind of mean. Dad says
he comes out here, he gets even meaner. Or a crazy
person gets crazier, a strong person gets stronger."

"You liked your dad, didn't you?"

"Sure. Everybody likes their dad."

"Not everybody, Reece."

"You mean you don't like your own dad?"

"Not very much. He's a real good man, I guess, but after Mom left . . ." She shook her head. "I think I reminded him of Mom too much. I favor her, you know."

"No, I didn't know that."

"Of course you didn't, Reece."

I said, "Where did your mom go?"

"She ran off with some umbrella salesman."

"Oh."

"Dad would say, 'You're just like your mother.' He'd say that all the time. And sometimes I'd catch him looking at me, and I'd know, I'd just know he was thinking about her."

I said, "Hmm," like I knew all about it.

"Maybe I am like Mom. Maybe Dad was right about that. I ran away, too, but I just couldn't stand it anymore. Do you think it works that way, Reece?"

"What do you mean?"

"Do you think that you end up being just like your parents?"

"No, I think you can be what you want to be."

"Maybe so." She snuggled closer and it was wonderful. I squeezed her a little, and she squeezed back. That was good too. Then she said, "I should get back downstairs, Reece."

I didn't move.

"Will you come and talk to me again sometime?"

"I sure will. I surely will do that."

I put on my shirt and boots. There was a lot more that I wanted to say to Kathryn, but I didn't know what it was. I put the rest of my poker money on her chest of drawers when I reached for my hat, my back toward her so she wouldn't see.

I opened the door and turned. "So long, Kathryn."

"So long, Reece."

When I closed the door, I thought about facing Fitsimmons and his buddies. When I thought about the questions they would ask, it made me mad. I looked down the hall for another way out. There were four other doors, but no outside steps.

I walked down the hall and poked my head around the corner. There they were, still playing cards. I was one step down when the front door opened and four men came in quickly, chased by blowing snow. It was one-eared Colby, Shorty, and two other men wearing badges on their coats.

Fitsimmons saw them, then glanced up at me at the top of the stairs. I backed up the stairs softly.

Kathryn had locked her door. I tapped it with a knuckle.

"Who's there?"

"It's me, Reece."

She opened the door and smiled in a glad-to-see-me way. I slipped inside and held her shoulders. "Is there another way out?"

"What?"

"I've got to run. Two of those guys I told you about are down there with the law. Is there a way out?"

"Come on." She was wearing her slip. I held her hand as she led me down the hall. She opened a door and peeked inside. "The window," she said.

I walked across the room and forced up the window. Cold air shocked the room. When I turned, Kathryn was holding her shoulders. "Go," she said. "Go, and come back."

I stepped out onto the tin roof that covered the boarded walkway. Kathryn reached up to close the window. I stuck my head back through. "Kathryn, could you do something else? I mean, is there something else you could do to make a living?"

She pushed at my head. "Mind your own business, Mr. Reece."

I pushed back against her. "I'll bet Mr. Fitsimmons would give you a job. You could work in his store."

She pushed harder. "You better go." She started lowering the window and I had to jerk my head out. My boots slipped on the snow cover, and I went down hard on my side and slid. My legs went over, but I managed to grab hold of the edge, hang for a moment, then drop to the ground.

The weather had cleared the street. I ducked my head against the blowing snow and headed for Fitsimmons's stables.

It was pitch-black, but Packy snorted for me and I found her inside a stall toward the back. I touched her muzzle and she nodded. I tossed on the blanket and saddle and knelt down to cinch up.

The stable door squeaked. "Reece?"

"Yeah, back here."

There was a scratch of a match, then yellow light. Fitsimmons held the lantern out to the side as he approached Packy and me. "You find all your gear?"

"Yeah. I think so." I tightened down the saddle cinch and tossed the reins over Packy's head. "The rest is in the hotel."

"I went up there first, looking for you. Brought your rifle and some bacon from the store." He sat the lantern on a hay bale and shrugged out of his parka. "You better take this, Reece."

"Thanks. Thanks a lot." I put on the heavy coat and buttoned up.

"Colby's telling a different story," Fitsimmons said. "He's saying you bushwhacked Marshal Combs and stole his money."

"Marshal Combs, is that the fat man?"

"I guess so. They brought the body in with them, but I didn't get a look at it. Shorty backs up Colby. Swears that's the way it happened." He shoved my rifle into the saddle sheath.

I led Packy out of the stall. "That's not true, Mr. Fitsimmons. It happened just like I told you."

"I know, son. I told the sheriff that very thing, but Colby and the short guy tell it different. It's your word again theirs, and they're wearing stars."

We headed toward the door. Fitsimmons stuffed a package into my saddlebag and blew out the lantern. "You think you can find that Injun, get him to back your story?"

"I don't know, Mr. Fitsimmons. I don't know, but I sure will try. They aren't going to look for him, are they?"

Fitsimmons said, "That's for sure." He opened the stable door and looked outside. "Mount up, Reece."

I climbed into the saddle. "Will you get my stuff from the hotel? Hold my fur money. I'll be back. Take out for the parka and the bacon."

"I'll do her, son." He pushed the door open.

"And give Kathryn a job, let her work in the store for you instead of what she's doing."

He smiled up at me and gave Packy a slap. She took a few steps, pranced at the snow, then walked up the alleyway. When we came to the end of the building, I touched her with my heels, and we hit the main street at a gallop, turning north.

There were shouts, and a "That's him" followed by pistol shots. Me and Packy had never been shot at before. She stretched it out, and we raced through the snow.

◆ 6 ◆

After a mile the heat of the gunshots wore down and I began to feel the cold. I let Packy slow to a canter and thought things over.

The cabin was about twenty miles from town, an easy four-hour journey in good weather. I wondered if the sheriff would give chase with the storm like it was. I turned and looked down. There was about two inches of snow, and Packy's hoofprints were easy to read. How long would it take the snow to cover them?

Two choices, both risky. I could try to make my cabin, or I could backtrail into town, hoping I could sneak into some shelter. I searched my mind for a third choice and came up empty. Dad used to read Shakespeare and quote from his books. One I remembered was, "There's little choice in rotten apples."

Packy heard them first and quickened her pace. I was so deep in thought that I hadn't heard the posse until they were much too close. It sounded like they were right on top of us. I asked Packy for some extra speed, and she opened her stride, and we flew through the snow. I don't know how she found her way at that speed, but she did.

I listened for the posse as we dashed through the storm and thought I heard them now and then. I couldn't be sure. They must have been able to read from Packy's tracks that they were close. I got low over Packy's neck, standing in the stirrups and letting my bent knees take the shock. She appreciated the help and smoothed into a racing stride.

Packy stopped so quickly that I almost went over her head. She went into a nervous prance and snorted at me. I squinted and tried to see ahead. "What is it, Packy?"

I jumped off and led her forward through the driving snow. It was a big cedar tree, blown over and slanting across the wagon trail. How did she know it was there?

"Good girl, Packy." I led her off to the right, and we traced our way up the bank, following the trunk. We both slipped and slid as we made our way around the mass of roots that had pulled up as the tree went down. Going back down the bank to the road was a little easier.

I put a foot in the stirrup and heard the posse coming hard. I drew my Winchester, worked the lever, and fired straight up in the air, holding the reins with my left hand. I jacked another shell and fired another warning shot. There were some shouts from the other side of the tree. One rider didn't pull up in time and I heard him crash into the tree. Branches cracked, and a heavy thud told me the horse was down.

Voices cut through the wind. A groan from the injured rider. I cupped my hands and shouted through the storm. "Go on back."

A pistol shot boomed, then a voice yelled, "Hold your fire, dammit!" There were some murmurs, then, "That you, Reece?"

"Yeah."

"Sheriff Ames. You're under arrest."

"How do you figure that?"

"I'm the sheriff and I say you're under arrest."

"What for?"

"For murderin'."

"I didn't kill that man, Sheriff. They're lying, those two, probably shot him themselves."

His voice came through the darkness. "Give yourself up. Come into town with us. We'll sort this out."

"No, thanks. I'm going to find a witness, then I'll be back."

Silence. "Hey, Reece?"

"What?"

"Thanks for the shots. That was fairly decent."

"You're welcome."

"I'll be coming for you when this storm blows out. You know that? Be better for you to give it up right here."

I eased into the saddle and slipped the Winchester into the scabbard. I leaned forward and put my arms around Packy's neck. "Let's go home, Packy."

A half hour later Packy found the turnoff and began climbing into the foothills. I tried to keep my toes moving, wiggling inside the boots. My hands were in my pockets, the reins looped around the saddle horn. I had been plenty cold before, but nothing like this. This was scary. I could actually die out here. I could die if the sheriff caught up with me. This morning I didn't have any worries. "Get us home, old girl."

We came to the top of the rise and Packy stopped, feeling for direction. The snow was coming harder, stinging my face and eyes. She made up her mind and worked her way through some trees, down a gentle hill. There was a new sound, a roar from straight overhead. It got louder and lower over the next few minutes, then the full force of the storm hit.

Packy plodded on through the gale. The snow was drifting into belly-high dunes that she had to heave and plow through. I tried to wiggle my toes again, and nothing happened. I couldn't tell if they were moving. I couldn't even tell if they were there. I had to pull my hand from the pocket to wipe crusted snow from my eyes. I pinched at my nose and felt nothing. I rubbed at it and after a while began to feel pain. A lot of pain.

Packy pushed on. I couldn't see the ground under my feet, but she was finding her way somehow. I wanted to make it for her sake as much as for my own. I kind of wanted to see that girl again too. How much farther? I tried to think back, figuring off miles in my head.

I jerked awake in time to grab the saddle horn and straighten up. Packy was high-stepping through another drift. I dipped out a double handful of snow from my lap and washed my face with it, spread and squeezed my eyes, and sucked icy air through my nose. Cold. So cold, so sleepy. Just thinking about sleep felt warm. Tempting. Deadly.

The storm beat at us. It seemed like something personal and deliberate. I couldn't fight back against it or reason with it. There was no place to hide. Wishing it would stop wouldn't help. The storm didn't care.

Packy was breathing in short bursts, making hoarse grunts when she blew out, then rasping in another lungful. She would kill herself at this rate. There was nothing I could do to help her. "You're on your own, Packy."

Sleep beckoned again with promises of warmth. I tried tensing muscles, my neck and arms. I made fists, shrugged my shoulders, tightened my belly, and squeezed against my chest muscles. I could feel Shanti's arrowhead, the only thing I could really feel. I squeezed my chest muscles again and felt a trace of warmth from the arrowhead.

Did Packy know the way, or was she just moving to keep my hopes up? I pulled some more warmth from Shanti's arrowtip. Imagination or not, it felt good.

Packy was on level ground, walking broadside to the wind. She would stagger when the stronger gusts hit us. She would grunt, take two steps, rasp, two steps, grunt, two steps, rasp, two steps, grunt. . . .

The stillness awakened me. Packy wasn't moving. The wind still howled, but I didn't feel it. I was almost glad that it was over, glad that Packy had given up before she went down. "Nice try, old girl."

I half fell off the saddle, holding to the horn for balance, trying to feel my legs. I didn't know if I was standing. I must have been standing but couldn't tell for sure. Packy lowered her head and turned toward me. I looked for her eyes, trying to focus. I blinked, blinked again, and saw them. Just to the left of her eyes was the stable door. I blinked again, and it was still there.

Home.

⭒ 7 ⭒

The stable door wouldn't budge. I yanked again and gained an inch, then another inch. No more. I dropped to my knees and scooped away snow with frozen fingers, trying to hate the snow away from the door.

I gripped the door again and heaved it open another few inches, then put my foot against the side of the stable and yanked again, lying on my back. Packy put her head and neck inside and stepped over me as she squeezed through.

I crawled in after her. There was no light in the stable. I used the inside wall to lean up to my feet and pull the door shut. So cold. So sleepy. Packy was standing by my side chugging in air. I reached a hand into the darkness and found her rump, traced her back with my other hand and found the cinch strap. Her saddle rolled off and hit the floor with a thump.

I leaned on Packy as we staggered to her stall. The blanket was where it should be, and I managed to get it draped over her. The stable was attached to the cabin, and the side door wasn't far away. Ten steps, over that way somewhere. My legs buckled under me, but I didn't know I was falling until I hit the floor and tasted dirt.

I wanted to stay right there and sleep. *Crawl. Move an arm, bring a leg forward, then the other arm. Do it again. Come on, Reece. You're almost there.* I had to stand to work the door latch, pushed forward, and fell into the cabin. I kicked the door shut. Sleep. I wanted to let go and sleep.

The wood stove was in the middle of the cabin and I crawled off in that direction. The air was colder than outside. No wind, just colder, a deadly stillness.

Did I lay a fire before I left? I always did, but I couldn't remember. Dad had said, "Always have a fire built before you leave." It was one of his rules.

Matches. Matches on the shelf by the bed. Have to crawl over to the right, feel for the shelf. If they were there, that's fine. If not I'll just sleep awhile, find them later.

I reached up to the shelf. My fingers didn't work. There was something on the shelf, but I couldn't pick it up. I brushed it off the shelf and heard it fall. It sounded like a box of matches. I had to use both hands to pick it up, pressing against the box with my palms. I held the matches against my chest and rolled toward the stove.

I was popping into sleep and jerking awake every second or two. I rolled again and came up against the stove. Now what? My mind waded through cold black syrup. The door, open the door.

I had to turn loose of the matchbox to pull open the door. It squeaked as it swung away. I palmed up the matchbox and fumbled with it. I couldn't feel with my fingers. There were matches in there. The box dropped to the floor, and I beat at it with my fist and mashed it with my palm.

The matches were loose on the floor now. *Think, Reece.* I got on my belly and licked the floor with my tongue until I found a match. I climbed to my knees, the match between my lips. I raised my hands to my mouth, worked the match between two shaking fingers of my right hand, and held the fingers shut with my left. I scratched the match against the side of the stove and it sparked into flame. My eyes were closed, but I saw the flame through my eyelids.

I opened my eyes. I had to squint and blink to bring the flame into focus. I moved my hand to the opening of the stove and saw a well-laid fire, dry leaves and pine kindling under pieces of split oak. "Good rule, Dad." The flame was against my fingers, but I couldn't feel it. I dropped the match onto the leaves and watched it sputter and nearly die. The side of a leaf smoked uncertainly over the tiny bead of match flame, then glowed, then burned.

I dropped off to sleep again and cracked my forehead against the side of the stove as I fell. It awakened me, but I knew it wasn't for long. The kindling had caught and was making crackling noises. It was dry heart pine slivers. I went to sleep and jerked awake in a second.

More to do. There were some hickory chunks at the side of the stove, and I added a few to the fire, swung the door shut, and pushed the latch down with my wrist. Sleep.

I rolled to the bed and reached an arm onto it and heaved up to my knees. My chest was on the bed. Almost there. *Boots.* Have to get the boots off. I managed to sit and haul my right leg across my left knee. The boot slid off and clunked to the floor. *Sleep.* The other boot came off. I dropped back on the bed, hauled the turned-back blankets over me, and scooted down. With my last movement I pushed the blankets over my head and let go.

I fell asleep then kept right on falling. It was like

dropping off a cliff, past sleep into something else, somewhere on the other side of sleep to a place I'd never been.

Things were different and strange, but I wasn't scared. For one thing it was nice and warm without being too hot. I just kind of floated around without being in a hurry to get anywhere. After a while I knew that I was moving, heading in a straight line through space. There were rounded walls all around, but they weren't really walls. It was dark, but there was light all around.

The sound was like that too. There was complete silence, but on the other side of the silence a quiet, high-pitched hum. It was the kind of hum you hear in your head if you listen real hard in the silence. I had heard it before and wondered about it.

Then Dad was there with me. Right there! It wasn't a shadowy dream figure, it was really him, the sense of him, the feel of him were there too. He looked a lot better than he had before he died. He was smiling, and I smiled back at him. We didn't say anything and didn't need to.

Grandma was in her rocking chair, just rocking back and forth like she used to do with me when I was a baby. I was still floating, but I could feel her arms around me, the softness of her breasts through the cotton dress.

The little boy I saw next was my brother, the one who had died the day he was born, ten years ago. I don't know how I knew he was my brother, but I knew, and it was a real sure knowing. We were going to have some good times together, my brother and me.

I floated by some other people, the old man who used to carve walking canes and tell me stories and the little girl who disappeared after a flood. I had helped look for her up and down the banks of the Ohio. I wished that I could tell her mother that she was safe and happy now.

Then they were all there together, and I was with them all, and I looked at everyone, one at a time at the same time. I know it doesn't make sense the way I tell it, but that's the way it was.

Then I was moving again, back the way I had come, pulled by many strings. There was some sadness as I watched them grow smaller in the distance. The sadness was mixed with a soft, peaceful joy.

✦ 8 ✦

Cold and dark, feet on fire.

Headache. Fingers stiff.

Thirsty, mouth dry. Tongue thick.

Pull down blankets to chin, open eyes. Darkness. Storm still howling outside. Cold. *Sleep some more.*

Packy. Got to see Packy.

I sat on the edge of the bed, put my feet on the floor, and tried to stand. I was dizzy in the darkness and had to drop back on the bed. When I stood again the dizziness wasn't as bad. I felt my way through the dark and found a candle on the table. I lit the candle, and the yellow light spread the room awake.

The fire had burned down to a few glowing coals. I must have slept about three hours. I raked the coals toward the front of the firebox, added pine kindling and oak sticks. The kindling was flaming when I added some split logs. I stuffed the stove full before closing the door and imagined the heat it would give.

I picked up two buckets and shuffled to the front door in stockinged feet. The storm was waiting, angry that I had escaped. I filled the buckets with packed snow from a drift on the porch and ducked back inside. It had taken less than a minute, but the storm had drained all warmth from my body. I put the buckets on the stove and stood close, hunching my shoulders and shivering.

I got the kerosene lamp lit, and the one-room cabin cozied up and felt warmer. I looked at the thermometer nailed to the wall. Forty degrees. It must have been about twenty outside. I found the ten-gallon washtub, carried it out to the front porch, and packed it with snow. I dragged it back inside. The two buckets had warmed the snow into a slushy mixture. I added more fresh snow from the tub and got a coffeepot and frying pan from the cabinet, filled them with snow, and placed them beside the two buckets, using all the surface space of the stove top.

I worked with the fire, adding a hickory log and a few smaller pieces. The snow had melted in the frying pan, and I poured the water into one of the buckets and filled all the containers with snow from the tub. When I dropped snow onto the stove top, it hissed and steamed in a very satisfactory manner.

I carried the lamp and a bucket of water out the back door into the stable. Packy turned to watch me and twitched her ears. I stroked her neck as she took some deep pulls. She raised her head and turned to nuzzle my side, then returned to drinking. I forked down some hay, and she was chewing steadily when I took the bucket back into the cabin.

I drank warm water from the pot, pulling it down greedily in gulps. I made one more trip to the porch for snow, filling all my pots, pans, and pails to the top. I carried another pail of water out to Packy and got Fitsimmons's bacon from the saddlebag. The thermometer read forty-five degrees now.

I put two cups of dried beans in the pot and covered

it with a lid, added grounds to the boiling water in the coffeepot, and let it roll for a minute before setting it on the table. While the grounds settled, I sliced off some thick bacon slabs. They sizzled when I dropped them in the skillet. It was a fine sound.

The coffee was wonderful. I turned the bacon with a fork and carried the cup in both hands to look at the thermometer again. Forty-eight degrees, almost forty-nine. I was alive and warm and safe. I would think about my other problems later.

And that dream. I felt like the dream had tried to tell me something, but I couldn't figure out what it was.

And Kathryn.

The beans were on a slow boil. I stirred them from the bottom, returned the lid, and lifted out a piece of bacon. It must have been an entire day since I had eaten, and the bacon went down in three quick swallows.

I made myself eat the second piece in slow nibbles. It would do more good that way. I poured some bacon grease in with the beans and moved the pot to the side of the stove top.

The headache was gone, but my body was still stiff and sore. My feet burned, especially at the toes. Later on I would take off my socks and look at them. Somehow I had to find Shanti and try to talk him into coming into town with me to testify to the sheriff. What if he didn't want to come? I'd worry about that later too. First thing to do was find him.

And then there was that dream to think about. I could still feel it, still see it.

The beans were softer. I sat the pot on the table to cool while I took off the parka. My thermometer said fifty-two degrees, and it felt like summer. I stretched the clothesline across the room in back of the stove and tossed the parka over it.

After a few spoons of beans the hunger pangs eased off. I put the ten-gallon tub on the stove and poured myself another cup of that good hot coffee. Between spoons of beans and sips of coffee I straightened up around the cabin. *How do you find one man in this big territory?*

I carried some water out to the stable. Packy understands what I say to her even if I don't say anything. I can just *think* things to her. I told her how much I loved her with my thoughts, and a feeling came back from her that I felt in the center of my chest. I patted her neck in the silent darkness.

Images from that dream slipped in and out of my mind. I wondered if it was really a dream or something else.

Fifty-six degrees. The water was steaming in the ten-gallon tub. I added a big hickory log and sat down on the bed and slipped off my socks. The tips of my toes were blue, but when I touched them the feeling was there. The knuckles at the base of my big toes were tender, and the ankles were stiff. I tossed the socks into the tub and stripped down to the skin. I added my shirt and BVDs to the steaming water and swished it all around, then wrung them out and spread them on my clothesline. The Levi Strauss pants went in last so the blue color could seep out.

I took a last look around the cabin before blowing out the lantern. I sat on the bed and held Shanti's arrowhead in my hand, searching for feelings in the candlelight. I thought of his face and listened for his voice in my head. "Leece," it said.

I blew out the candle and pulled up the covers. It had been nice with Kathryn in my arms. She was so soft. Slender yet soft at the same time. It would be nice if she was here with me now.

9

Silence woke me. The storm had passed, and the window was bright with frosted sunlight.

I tossed some sticks in the fire and tried to guess how long I had slept. Four hours? Five? The clothes were dry, and I got into socks and BVDs. The sheriff and posse would be on their way soon. Maybe they were already on their way.

It didn't take long to fix a quick breakfast of bacon, rewarmed beans, and fried sourdough biscuits. Beans are better after they cool and you heat them up again. I took off Shanti's arrowhead and laid it on the table so that I could look at it while I ate. I picked the arrowhead up by the leather necklace, holding it at the knot and watching it swing gently back and forth. "Where are you, Shanti?" I whispered.

I bit into a biscuit. The arrowhead seemed to pause, hang uncertainly, then begin to swing in a new direction, toward the northeast. I held the arrowhead with my palm, then released it. It hung there for a moment, making up its mind, then began the northeast swing again. I put the necklace over my head. There were rugged mountains in that direction.

I put on another pair of socks, two pair of pants, two shirts and the parka. I cleaned out the coals and ashes and laid a new fire in the wood stove.

Dad had shown me how to make waterproof matches. He melted paraffin wax in a pot over low heat, then poured the liquid over a boxful of matches. After the wax cooled and set, he would slice off a few to carry in wet weather. There was a half box of waxed matches left, and I used my knife to carve off a chunk.

Packy was out of her stall, waiting for me. I flipped on her blanket and saddle, cinched down the strap, and took the saddlebags back into the cabin. My coffeepot, a pan, along with grounds, bacon, flour, and beans went into the saddlebags. I put together a bedroll and sat down to write a note.

Sheriff

I did not kill that man. I have never killed anybody. He was alive the last time I saw him. I bet the one-ear guy and short guy did him in. When I find the boy they were about to hang, I will bring him to town. He will tell you like I did. Do not trail me, or I will shoot at you.

Reece

I read the note over several times. It would have to do. I made up my bed so the sheriff could see I wasn't a bum, then led Packy out the stable door.

It was hushed quiet. The sun was bright and the sky was clear blue with some trails of scattered clouds that were high up. Things looked brittle and white, like the inside of an eggshell. The snow squeaked underfoot. I swung up into the saddle, stroked Packy's neck, and we moved off. I kept the morning sun behind my right shoulder.

Packy got a sense of our direction and found the easiest way, skirting the deeper drifts. The sunlight off the snow hurt my eyes, and I rode most of the time with eyelids shut. I pulled the neckerchief up to cover my mouth and nose. It cut the sharpness of the cold air a bit and made breathing easier.

After an hour I turned in the saddle to check our backtrail. Our tracks were deep and straight. I searched my mind for a way to hide our trail and throw off trackers.

It would take the sheriff an entire day to reach our cabin. He and the posse would probably spend the night, then follow me in the morning. I had a day's lead on them but kept looking back now and then anyway. I figured I might as well get into the habit. I was going to have to think like an outlaw for a time.

Toward midday we rode to the base of a cliff. Packy stopped and pulled at some dry grass. The cliff had sheltered the area from the storm. The ground was bare of snow for a hundred feet from the cliff's base. I climbed down and flipped the reins over Packy's head so that she could graze on the tufts of winter grass.

While the coffeepot full of snow thawed and heated over the fire, I dragged over a big hunk of pine log to sit on. I laced a slice of bacon over a sharpened stick and held it over the flames. The dripping grease made the fire spit and flame up.

When the bacon was done, I turned my back to the fire and looked things over between bites. A fire doesn't warm you as well when you don't look at it. We would have to skirt around that cliff face to continue our northeast journey, and one way looked as good as the other. If

I could slow down the posse for a few hours it might make a difference later on.

I finished the bacon, built up the fire, and hauled over another log, laying it about ten feet from the fire. I lifted some burning sticks and placed them around the second log and rolled my sit-down log on top of the first fire. The posse would think that I had slept between the two burning logs. At least I hoped they would. They would think they were close behind me, and maybe they would get careless and fall for a false trail I planned to put down.

I chopped down a small cedar tree with my knife and whistled Packy over. We rode off to the east, dragging the cedar behind us on a short line. After a hundred yards I turned toward the cliff, dragging the cedar like a big sweep broom.

Ten feet from the base of the cliff I turned west, and we rode for half a mile, keeping the cliff face on our right. The ground was frozen rock hard. I dismounted, untied the cedar, and pushed Packy toward the cliff base. I carefully swept away at our tracks and pushed Packy on ahead, staying right next to the cliff while I brushed behind her. We kept this up for a mile, past our first turn before I remounted and dragged the cedar behind us again. All that took an hour, and I may have been wasting my time. Packy thought so. Still, I felt better about making it harder for them. At least they would know they weren't following some dumb kid.

We were riding through deeper snow again. I untied the cedar tree and stuck it upright in the snow. I had to pass water and looked around for a good place, but there wasn't any. It was a solid white blanket of snow in all directions. Since there was no place to hide it, I unbuttoned my pants and drew a yellow arrow in the snow, pointing north.

The sun was behind us now, shining over my left shoulder as we climbed into the hills. I had no idea where Shanti was or what I would say if I found him. I thought it over while Packy found her way up through the trees and around the large outcrops of boulders. She seemed to have an idea of where to go.

As we rode along I got to thinking about Dad again. Dad had talked a lot during his last days. It was amazing how much he left for me to think about. There was a lot of quiet time after he died. I would think over the things he had said while I rode from one place to another, checking our traps.

Sometimes the fever would take him and he would ramble on, half out of his head, not making any sense. Then he would come out of it and say things that he must have thought about for a long time. I think he knew he was dying. He kept saying he felt better and would be on his feet in a day or two, but I think he knew. I knew too. It was the worst thing there ever was.

"You haven't had a chance to grow up like a boy should," Dad said one evening. "Not much schooling except what I could teach you. Nobody your own age to play with, no girls to chase around. Been hard for you, I know that."

"No. I like it here, Dad. And you've taught me—"

Dad held up a hand. "You've become a man any father would be proud of." He had to stop talking to cough for a while. I thought he would never stop, but he finally did. After he got his breath, he said, "I know you're a man, but I don't think you know it yet. Sooner or later you'll have to prove it to yourself, to others. I know you'll be up to it." He coughed some more, then fell into a fever sleep.

Packy pushed on. The climb was getting steeper. I guess this was it, the time to prove it. I thought over the last two days and wondered if I should have let the lynchers have their way and minded my own business.

Dad used to read the Bible a lot and tell me stories from it. He said it was a good book but that it was much too long. "A man don't need to know all this stuff to be a good man, all the begats and Sodomites and cubits and everything. He just needs to know one thing."

I said, "What's that?"

"Always do what's right," Dad said. "Remember that, always do what's right."

"Yes, sir."

"Of course, doing the right thing is the easy part," Dad said. "The hard part is knowing what is right sometimes."

"How can you tell, Dad?"

"You can't," he said. "Not every time. Sometimes you kind of have to trust your feelings."

I thought about the lynchers and about Shanti, his face and smile and the way we talked. I remembered trading gifts with him and the way he looked at me and said my name, "Leece." As near as I could tell, I had done what was right. It had brought a whole lot of trouble with it, but when I thought about it some more, I got a feeling that things would work out. If I had turned away from the trouble, I wouldn't like myself for it. Being able to like yourself is worth something.

There was something about that dream that made me feel better too.

We crossed deer tracks, two does and a buck. It was a fresh trail, quartering off to the left. I let Packy walk in their hoof prints and they led us through a narrow pass formed by a fault in a large rock formation. It was a shortcut, a narrow hallway with steep rock walls. If the posse missed it, I would gain some more time on them. More outlaw thinking. Reece the outlaw.

I was feeling the cold more than I should have. Riding through the blizzard had drained something out that I hadn't put back in. There was more than an hour of daylight left, but I found a good campsite beneath an overhang rock shelf and got busy setting things up. I used my rope to drag over two big logs from trees that had fallen last year, then took off Packy's saddle.

It was cozy and growing warmer under the rock shelf after I got a big fire blazing. The coffee began warming me from the inside. Packy had strolled over to a stand of pines and was finding some dry grass under their branches. I watched the daylight fade as bacon fried and beans boiled. It was a good camp.

I ate slowly, squatting by the fire, a blanket wrapped over my shoulders. I felt like the only person on earth under a clear sky full of stars. I didn't feel like a man at all, more like a boy who was lonely and scared. I finished eating, dressed up the fire, and rolled up in my blanket. I watched the flames until my eyes got bleary, and would have cried if I thought it would have done any good.

☙ 10 ❧

In the morning Shanti's arrowhead wanted to go straight
north. I hung the necklace from a branch and watched it
swing, first this way, then that way. When I held it with
my fingertips, it went back to its northern swing. It
wasn't much to go on, but it was all I had so I put my
trust in it.

It was tough going for Packy. There were fewer
drifts, but the footing was treacherous over hard scrabble
rocks. I had to dismount and lead her over a few places,
and toward noon we came to a sheer rock face that a
mountain goat couldn't have climbed. We had to back-
track, losing time as we retraced our steps down the hillside.

A big hawk sailed overhead, making its whistle cry
every few seconds. I whistled back to it. If I had the
hawk's view of things, I could find my way up this mountain. I tried it, shutting my eyes and imagining the way
things looked from the sky. I got a picture in my mind of
me and Packy trailing down the hill, two black dots
against the snow. The rock face was behind us and, over
to our right about a mile away, a pass. I opened my eyes
and headed Packy in that direction.

The pass was there. I searched the sky for the hawk, but it was gone. I sent it my thanks anyway. The snow was deeper again, and we were in shadows as the sun lowered to the west over my left shoulder. It would be nice to sleep in a bed, under blankets with a fire in the stove. It would be nice to sleep with Kathryn.

Packy almost stepped on the rabbit before it bolted and ran off to the right. I pulled the Winchester from the scabbard, levered a shell, and snapped off a quick shot. Snow spurted in front of the rabbit, and it cut to its left. I made up my mind, took a breath, and rolled it with my next shot. He did a somersault and slid onto his side. By the time we had walked up to him he had quit kicking.

Dad always had me do any shooting that had to be done because I was so good with the rifle. Dad said I was the best natural rifle shot he had ever seen. He also said I was the worst he had ever seen with a handgun. I just could never get the hang of it. Dad laughed about it and gave up trying to teach me. "You'd be better off throwing rocks," he said.

One day we had surprised the pair of wolves that had been raiding our traps. Wolf pelts brought good money, and there was a big bounty on them, too. I shot the first one from the saddle. The other wolf was running full out. I jumped from the saddle, lay belly flat, and brought it down with a very long shot.

Dad counted paces as we walked up to the carcass. "Hundred eighty-three yards," he said. "That was some shot." He slapped my shoulder. The wolf was a beautiful animal in prime shape. It was so still in the snow. Still forever, a trickle of blood dripped from its mouth. The eyes were open and staring.

Dad said, "You don't take much pleasure from this, do you, son?"

"What do you mean?"

"I can see it in your face. You're a hell of a shot for a boy who hates killing."

"I don't hate it, Dad."

"Sure you do. Nothing wrong with it neither. I sorta like you that way. You ever start taking pleasure from it, I'd worry about you. It's your nature to be gentle, and I don't want you to turn from it."

He pulled his knife and began field-dressing the wolf. I said, "Does it ever bother you, Dad?"

"Yep." He sawed a long cut down the wolf's belly, reached in, and pulled out the entrails. "Whatever it was that made you and me made these animals. I figure they got the same feelings you and I do. Some of them, anyway." He opened the chest cavity and pulled out the lungs and the heart. When the heart hit the snow it pumped twice.

I thought about the things Dad had said while I turned the rabbit on a spit between two forked branches. While the coffee boiled, I melted snow in the cook pot for Packy. I set the coffeepot off the flames and tested the snow water with my fingers.

Packy drank it down. I filled the pot with more snow and set it over the flames. The rabbit was almost done. I put a handful of dried beans in my hat and walked over to Packy with it. She bent her head to sniff at the beans, then looked up at me, right in the eyes.

"I know, Packy. Eat them anyway. It's the best I can do."

She lowered her head again, took another whiff, and looked at me again before she lipped out a few beans and began chewing. Packy likes beans well enough. She just wanted me to know that it wasn't her favorite. She took a bigger mouthful and began grinding them up after she had made her point.

The rabbit was tough and stringy, but the chewing was good. There was a half moon slipping in and out of the blowing night clouds. A wolf howled from the distance, off to the east. Another wolf answered from the north.

I had plenty of firewood, but it was all small sticks, none bigger than my wrist. I sat up eating the rabbit meat slowly and trying to make it last, sucking the bones clean and feeding the fire. I thought about Kathryn some, the way she felt under my hands, the way she smiled at me. When I thought of her being with someone else it made my chest get tight, and I had to think of other things real fast.

Maybe Kathryn's dad went kind of crazy, thinking about his wife being with the umbrella man.

I leaned back against the saddle and tossed some more pine sticks on the fire. The two rabbit legs were left, and I warmed one on the end of a stick. A shooting star fell silently off to my right, blazing a streak through the blackness, then winking out suddenly, silently. I wondered how many people had seen that. What kind of people and what were they thinking about now?

I saved a rabbit leg for morning, built up the fire, and lay back, resting my head against the saddle. I decided that I wouldn't go upstairs with Kathryn when I saw her again. We would do something else, maybe rent a buggy and take a ride. I tried to think of how to ask her. "I would like the pleasure of your company . . ." sounded too much like the Englishmen in the books Dad had me read. I turned on my side and looked at the flames. "Would you care to accompany me . . . ?" I closed my eyes. Just before I dropped off to sleep, I decided on "Wanna take a ride?"

Packy whinnied softly, and I popped awake, feeling cold. The fire had burned down to a bed of coals. The moon was setting in the west, and the night was darker, full up with vague shapes and a nervous silence. I sat up and threw tinder on the fire. Packy whinnied again, like she was frightened too.

There was a sound off to my left, a little quick sound, then dead quiet again. I listened hard to my own heartbeat and pulled the Winchester to me and listened some more. Nothing.

I remembered the sound in my mind, trying to place it, locate it. I pulled the rifle under the blanket and worked the lever action slowly. The click was too loud and snapped through the brittle night air. My hands were sweating. I made myself let out some air. Packy was off to my right and upwind, standing still in the fading moonlight.

I took another breath and fed the fire, acting natural. Was I being watched? I felt around me for a presence, for anything. I picked up my cooking stick and held the rabbit leg over the flames. After it warmed, I took a bite. I didn't have any spit and had to chew it up dry.

I felt eyes on me from off to my left and focused my attention there. Packy took a nervous step to the side. Her ears were up. So were mine.

I knew the voice was coming before he spoke.

"Don't move, son. We're coming to your fire."

·11·

Four shapes appeared from the darkness and stood in the edge of firelight. There was a click of a gun cocked close behind me. That made five altogether.

I said, "Good morning."

A figure stepped closer. His star caught the firelight. I pulled my Winchester from under the blanket and held it out to him, stock first. He holstered his pistol. "Sheriff Ames," he said. "And you're damn well under arrest this time."

I said, "You want some coffee?"

"I sure do."

"Me too." It was Mr. Fitsimmons, and it sure felt good to see him. The dumb guy was there, too, along with One-Eared Colby and Shorty. The other man was an Indian dressed in soldier clothes. They gathered around and held their palms toward the fire.

Dawn was working its way up over the eastern horizon. I said, "You must have tracked me all night?"

Sheriff Ames said, "Yep." He jabbed a thumb toward the Indian. "Old Dan don't need much light."

The Indian said, "I follow piss arrow." He smiled at me and I smiled back at him.

As the water heated, the dumb guy brought up their horses. The men left the fire one at a time to bring cups and plates. Fitsimmons took care of the cooking while I told the sheriff my side of the story. He watched my face and listened closely.

The coffee was boiling hot. When I was through the sheriff took a noisy sip, holding his cup in both hands. Fitsimmons said, "That's the way he told it to me. Exactly the same way."

Colby said, "He's lying." He said it softly.

"That's right," Shorty said. "He's a liar."

Fitsimmons said, "Lying man usually don't keep his story straight, twicet in a row."

Fitsimmons had bacon frying and a pot of rice on boil. Sheriff Ames said, "I gotta search through your kit, Reece."

"Go ahead."

Fitsimmons said, "That Indian from around here somewhere?"

I said, "I don't know." I started to tell him about taking my direction from the arrowhead, but thought it would sound foolish. The tracker stared at me. I reached inside my shirt and pulled Shanti's arrowhead necklace over my head and handed it to him. "My friend Shanti gave this to me."

He held the arrowhead in his palm and looked it over, rubbing his thumb over the sides. "This a fine kind of Indian man." He handed it back to me and said, "Stand."

I stood up. Dan lifted two sticks from the fire and stood facing me. He held the flaming ends between us, one to each side and searched my face with a steady gaze.

He turned away and walked to Colby. "Stand."

Colby said, "Get away from me." He waved an arm at him.

The sheriff came back to the fire. He said, "Do what he says, Colby. Won't hurt nothin'."

Colby laid down his coffee and stood with his hands in his back pockets. Dan looked at him the way he had looked at me. He turned to Shorty, "You stand."

"I don't take no orders from no Injun," Shorty said.

Sheriff Ames said, "Do it, Sam."

Fitsimmons handed me a plate with bacon and rice steaming from it. We watched Dan look at Shorty, and Shorty didn't take to it. After a moment he turned, spit, and sat back down. "Enough a that," he said.

Fitsimmons passed plates all around, and spoons clicked and scraped against the tin. Shorty spilled some rice on his lap and said curse words. The dumb guy belched and grinned at all of us. Dan ate slowly, looking from Colby to Shorty as he chewed. After a moment he began to smile at some secret thought.

Sheriff Ames said, "What do you say, Dan?"

Dan looked at the sheriff, chewed some more, then laid his plate down. He held his hand toward me, "Straight tongue, true eyes." He turned toward Colby and Shorty. "Crooked tongue, eyes like snake go through sand." He made a wiggle-waggle motion with his hands.

Colby looked at Dan through half-closed eyes, the muscles in his jaws working. Shorty said, "What do you expect from a damn Injun, huh? What do you think he'd say?"

Sheriff Ames said, "Dan's usual right on these things."

Fitsimmons said, "Boy's always been real straight with me, like his dad."

The dumb guy said, "What's Dan mean, 'Like snake go through sand'?"

The sheriff said, "He means that those two are lying, the kid's telling the truth."

"Well, shoot," the dumb guy said, "I coulda told you that."

I helped myself to some more rice and bacon. Fitsimmons winked at me. I said, "Thanks for coming, Mr. Fitsimmons."

He poured my cup full. "I didn't have much choice," he said. "Kathryn made me. Kathryn and Cora."

"Really?" I put down my cup and took a bite of rice. "How is Kathryn?"

"She's . . . she'll be okay."

"What do you mean, will be?"

Fitsimmons dropped his head to his chest. "She's all right, Reece. It's just . . . well, Colby roughed her up a little is all, 'cause she helped you get away."

I didn't even think about it. My dive carried me across the fire and into Colby's chest, bowling him over. I tumbled past him, scrambled to my feet, and charged into him again before he could stand. I ended up on top of him this time and got a fist into his face before he rolled me off. Before I could get to him again, he drew his gun.

"Don't do it, Colby." The sheriff had his gun pointed, held steady. He looked like a man who would shoot.

Colby thought it over, then crammed his pistol into his holster. "Keep him off a me. Keep him off, or I'll kill him."

"Take his gun, Dan. Take his buddy's gun too."

Shorty said, "What'd I do?"

The sheriff said, "I don't know what you did, you or

Colby or Reece either, for that matter. Near as I can figure, I got three suspects and one dead marshal. We'll go back and let the judge pick through it."

Fitsimmons put a hand on my shoulder. "It'll work out all right, Reece."

"Did he hurt her?"

"Slapped her some in the face. Eyes and mouth is kinda swole up. Probably turned blue by now, but no bones is broke or nothing."

"I'm going to kill Colby."

"You might have to."

Colby and Shorty were sitting on the other side of the fire, their plates in their laps. "What else do you guys do?" I said at them, and they both looked up. "You slap around little girls and whip somebody all tied up. What else? Break puppies' legs? Kick old ladies?"

Colby pointed his fork at me. "I'm going to hurt you real bad, kid."

"You want to try it now?"

He shook his head. "I want you to think about it."

We dressed up camp and mounted up. Dan led the way, followed by the dumb guy, Colby, Shorty, and Mr. Fitsimmons. The sheriff rode along beside me. It was another clear, crisp day. After a while Sheriff Ames asked, "You have any idea why they'd want to kill Marshal Combs?"

"No, sir. Do you believe it was them killed him?"

Sheriff Ames shrugged deeper into his coat. "Not my job. Up to the judge."

We rode a ways in silence. I said, "What's it like? What happens with the judge?"

"Well, everybody sits around a room, and the judge sits up in front behind a desk. He'll say something like, 'The People versus Reece on the charge of murder.'"

"What people?"

"I don't know. It's just what he says."

We rode past the place where I had shot the rabbit. I asked, "Then what?"

"I guess I'll be first," the sheriff said. "I'll have to tell the judge how Colby and Little Sam came in with Marshal Combs's body, saying you the one done it. Then I'll tell how we chased you when you ran and how we tracked you down."

"Then what?"

"He'll call the other witnesses. Colby and Little Sam. They'll tell the judge how it happened, how they say it happened. Then he'll ask you to talk, and you can tell your side."

It made me nervous to think about it. Colby and Shorty would have practiced their lies by then. There would be two of them, two grown men with one story. All I could do was tell my side, the truth. I said, "What do you think will happen, Sheriff?"

"Hard to say, boy. A lot depends on the judge, what kind of mood he's in, how much he's been drinking."

"What's the worst thing that could happen?"

The sheriff glanced over at me. He pulled his coat tighter and tucked his chin inside the collar. "Worst would be hanging."

I tried to swallow.

" 'Course, you being young and all, never in trouble before, he might just send you to the penitentiary for a few years."

There's little choice in rotten apples, I thought.

✦12✦

Our party had strung out with Dan and the dumb guy in the lead. Colby and Shorty were behind them, a dozen yards ahead of me and Mr. Fitsimmons. The sheriff rode ten paces behind.

Fitsimmons tore off a chew of jerky. "Kathryn told me about you asking her to go to work for me, quit whoring. Said I should tell you to take care of your own self. Madder'n hell now, you telling her what to do. She got the red ass you leaving her extra money, too. Never saw nobody so all fired mad."

"What's she mad about? I just thought, I mean I couldn't stand to think about her with someone like those two." I pointed up ahead at Colby and Sam.

"She sure called you some bad-awful names." Fitsimmons shook his head back and forth. "Little girl like her shouldn't know that kind of talk. I told her so, and now she's mad at me too."

"How come she asked you to come look for me, then?"

"She said somebody had to see after you. Said you was such a baby, you needed looking after." Fitsimmons swallowed his jerky and replaced it with a chaw of tobacco. He got it worked into his cheek real proper. "Kathryn's gone sweet on you, Reece."

"Sweet on me? I thought you said she was mad."

"She is. That's the way they work, women. Especially you tell them to do something they already know they should be doing. Women, they know you're right really gives them the reds."

"You think she'll quit the other, then, go to work for you?"

"She might, Reece." He swapped his chaw from right cheek to left. "What she'll do is, she'll study on it, and if she can make it seem like her own idea 'stead of yours, she just might do her. Won't never do it, though, if it looks like it's 'cause you told her to."

"That doesn't make any sense, Mr. Fitsimmons."

"Makes sense you know women," he said. "Perfect good sense." He worked up a spit and let fly. "Women are a funny thing, Reece. Can't never hope to understand them. Told my wife about it. How Kathryn being so mad, and she said she didn't blame her. Women know things, they know things about each other. It's a tit thing."

"A what?"

"A tit thing. They pass it along through the titty, mother to daughter."

"Women are real soft, Mr. Fitsimmons. Smooth and soft."

"Some of them are." He reached over to slap me on the shoulder. "You go on, I'm going to talk with Ames awhile."

I rode alone, with the sheriff and Fitsimmons behind me. I could hear their voices, but couldn't make out the words. I looked around, glancing one way, then the other, without turning my head, looking for a way to make a run for it. I didn't have a plan, but if I got a chance to get away, I was going to take it.

A quick flash of light, like a piece of the sun, stabbed my eyes from the rock peak up ahead. It came and went quickly. It was there, then gone in an instant. No one else had seen it, and we plodded along. There wasn't much taste to the jerky, but it gave me something to do.

Little Sam looked back over his shoulder, spoke to Colby, and reined in his mount. Colby kept riding while Little Sam waited. When I came up to him, he said, "You ever see a hanging, boy?"

"No."

"What they do is they drop a little trap door out from under you and you fall for a few feet. There's some slack in the rope. Sometime you can hear it when the neck bone cracks. But sometimes it don't crack, and the guy, he just chokes to death, kicking and jerking and pissin' his pants. How'd you like to do that?"

I said, "You've seen some hangings, huh?"

"I seen my share."

"Which do you like better, watching a hanging or whipping a man that's tied up?"

"You got me wrong, sonny. Whipping that Injun was just doing my job."

"That don't make it right, calling it your job."

"I was just trying to get the truth out of him."

"Truth about what?"

"You know."

We rode along in silence. Packy didn't like Little Sam's horse. Sam said, "That Injun showed you the map, didn't he?"

I didn't say anything. Little Sam said, "That's why you come up this way, ain't it? 'Cause he showed you that map."

I said, "I know why you like to watch hangings, why you like to whip somebody."

"Huh?"

"I just figured it out. You like it 'cause it's not you getting whipped, it's not you getting hung. Makes you feel like you're better than those guys."

Little Sam said, "Which one of these mountains the Indian come from? Tell me that and we'll change our story. We'll just say we found the marshal's body. Don't know who kilt him."

"Doesn't work, though, I bet."

"What doesn't work?"

"The feeling. I'll bet after a while it wears off and you know you're still a pig's ass. Then you need something else to get that feeling back."

"You don't know nothin'."

"I know more than you."

"Wasting my time with you," Sam said. "Wasting my time with a damn snot-nosed kid." He slapped at his horse and rode on up to join Colby. Packy felt easier with him gone.

Dan found the crack in the rock face, and we closed up and started through single file. There wasn't much light at the bottom between the sheer rock walls. Packy had her ears up, and I could feel her go tense between my legs. I patted her neck.

I could see the opening over Shorty's head as I rode behind him. His horse was balking and tossing its head. He jerked on the reins and kicked its sides with his heels, cursing it on through into the daylight.

A young Indian man appeared from the left, grabbing the reins of Shorty's horse with one hand. He held a rifle in his right hand pointed at Shorty's chest. I rode on through, and Shanti grabbed Packy's reins and led her off to the side, smiling up at me.

Other braves took Fitsimmons and Sheriff Ames by surprise too. They had brought off the ambush without firing a shot or saying a word. They got our party disarmed and off horses with hand gestures and grunts. I slid off the saddle. Shanti said, "Leece." We grabbed each other, hands on shoulders, and I said, "Shanti." He wore my neckerchief across his brow. It still looked real good on him.

There were a dozen or so young warriors. They had everyone back up against the rock face and sit down. Two braves stood over them with rifles while the others went through their saddlebags and bedrolls, laughing and talking as they scattered gear around on the snow.

I motioned for Shanti to come with me and we walked over to the row of new prisoners. I said their names as I pointed. "Sheriff Ames, Colby, Little Sam, Fitsimmons, Dan." I asked the dumb guy what his name was.

"Biggs," he said.

I asked Dan, "Can you talk with Shanti?"

Dan spoke, and Shanti answered. Dan nodded at me. "Shanti is of the Yahi tribe. I have some words same."

"Get him to tell what happened. Shanti talk to Dan, Dan talk to sheriff."

It took a while. While Shanti and Dan talked and gestured, the other braves gathered around and listened. Every minute or so Dan would tell the sheriff what Shanti had said so far.

Shanti told that he and two other braves had ridden to the fort to try to make peace. They were an advance party and carried a map to a gold cave that his Yahi tribe knew about. They had given the commander some chunks of gold and shown him the map. The map wouldn't do any good by itself, not without a man from their village to guide them part way. They wanted to trade the location of the gold for land for his people. The commander of the fort had agreed, and they would return with the chief and "touch the pen"—Dan's way of saying "sign a treaty."

Shanti said the three white men had followed them from the fort and shot his two companions in the back. They shot his horse and found the map he was carrying. He didn't understand their questions, but thought they wanted him to tell them where the gold cave was. Shanti said he would die before betraying his people. That is when Sam whipped him.

He told the rest of it about the same way that I had. Sheriff Ames listened closely. He asked Colby, "What do you two birds have to say now?"

"You've heard our story," Colby said.

Dan spoke to Shanti, and Shanti removed his buckskin shirt. His cuts had closed over. As he turned around we all saw the criss-cross whip slashes, each heavily scabbed. He was going to have a lot of scars.

I saw a dirty smile play across Sam's face when he saw those slash marks, and it made my blood go hot. I went over to his horse and snatched the whip off the saddle. It took me a few tries before I made it crack in the air. "Come on, Sam. It's payback time." I swung the whip around my head.

The Yahi braves backed away from the whip swing. I got another loud crack out of it. Sam's eyes were plenty scared. He pushed back against the rock, but the mountain didn't give any. I told Dan, "Tell them to drag him out here in the open."

Dan spoke to the braves, but Shanti said something

and they kept their places. Shanti stepped over to me and talked some more. Then he reached for the whip.

Dan said, "Shanti say you brave man, a spirit brother. Little man coward, heart like a small girl. You whip small one and you are coward. Shanti say he no brother to coward."

I looked at Shanti. "I want to hear him tell the truth, just one time."

Shanti shook his head, and we looked at each other for a minute. He reached out and touched my arrowhead, then his headband, then patted his chest over his heart. I knew what he meant and felt pretty foolish. My mad had wore off some by that time, and I don't think I could have whipped him anyway. I remembered Dad's words, "Always do what's right." I nodded to Shanti and dropped the whip. He picked it up and walked off.

Sheriff Ames said, "What are you going to do, Reece?"

"I don't know," I said. "What would you do?"

"Not my choice," Ames said. "You're holding the cards now, it's your play."

I thought about it. "What would you do, Mr. Fitsimmons?"

He shrugged his shoulders and shook his head. "Like Ames says, it's you holding the cards. One thing, I'd like to get out of here with my scalp. Cora needs me to look after her, and these Yahi boys keep eyeing my pretty curls."

Biggs said, "Let the Injuns take these two and hang 'em," he pointed toward Colby and Sam. "They're not worth a turnip nohow, and then there won't be nobody to testify agin you."

Biggs wasn't as dumb as I had thought.

I said, "How does that sound to you, Sam? You ever

watch a man hang? Not a pretty thing to see, the way I hear it. Sometimes the neck bone don't crack and the guy chokes, kicking and jerking."

Little Sam whispered something to Colby, and Colby shook his head no.

Sheriff Ames said, "Think about this, Reece. You get your friend here to come into town with us, he can back up your story for the judge."

"What if the judge doesn't believe us? It would be us two against those two."

"I can't promise nothing, but I believe you and I'll say so under oath."

Fitsimmons said, "Me, too, Reece."

Biggs said, "And me."

I looked at Dan. He nodded, just barely moving his head.

Shanti had walked off to the left and out of sight. I said, "Let me think about it," and walked away to find him. He was sitting on a flat-topped boulder staring out at the the rolling hills below. He turned around when he heard me approach. Our eyes met. After a moment he moved over a foot or so to make room for me beside him.

We shared the view together. It felt good, being with him again. After a few minutes I pointed at him, then myself, then south toward Macland. He looked into my eyes for a long moment, then pointed to me, to himself, and gestured toward the northwest.

I shook my head and repeated my gestures, pointing to Shanti, myself, and to the south. He stood and pointed to me, himself, and the northwest. I got to my feet. "Shanti, Reece," I said, pointing toward Macland. Shanti was giving me a frowning, angry look. I frowned back at him and we stood face-to-face for a long moment

before a smile began to work on his face. I tried to hold
back my own smile, but it broke through anyway.

Shanti stooped down and picked up some small
rocks. He sorted through them and dropped all but two.
He held up a dark-colored pebble and pointed to the
northwest. Then he held up a light stone and pointed to
the south. I nodded.

Shanti put his hands behind his back. I heard the
stones click together as he shook them. He stuck his
arms out to me, his hands clenched into fists. I looked at
his eyes, searching for a clue then touched his left hand.
He opened his fingers. The brown stone was in his palm.
We were riding north.

·13·

The warriors laid all the guns on a blanket, rolled it up, and tied the ends. I shook hands with Sheriff Ames, Biggs, Dan, and Mr. Fitsimmons. "If I can talk him into it, I'll bring Shanti into town to talk to the judge."

Sheriff Ames climbed onto his saddle. "What if he won't come in?"

"I don't know, Sheriff. I don't know what I'll do then. But it'd sure be dumb to just give myself up and get hung. You wouldn't do that, would you?"

"No, but then I wouldn't ride off with a bunch of wild Indians neither."

Mr. Fitsimmons said, "I'll hold your money and your kit. Come in and clear your name. Don't let these two run you."

Four braves rode off with the sheriff and his party, carrying the blanketful of guns. We watched them until they were out of sight, then mounted and rode north. The man that led the way was tall and slender with a real big nose.

After an hour we came to a shallow stream about five steps across. Big Nose got halfway across, then reined his horse to the right, going upstream and staying in the middle. I could see up ahead where it came tumbling out of a split in the mountain.

When we got to the split, the gravel bottom turned rocky, and Packy had some trouble finding her purchase on the round boulders. So did the Indian's horses, but they made it through, and Packy wasn't going to be out-done.

It was more boulders for fifty paces before the stream mellowed out to a gravel bottom again. It ended in a spring pool of blue-green water that looked deep. I won-dered where we would go now. The banks were steep-sloped with no sign of a trail.

Big Nose got off his horse and led it up the left-hand bank. The others followed, and so did Packy and I. There was a good bit of slipping and jerking of bridles. I followed them up the hillside as best I could, and they waited for us at the top. Shanti motioned with his hands for me to hurry.

We heaved our way up, and several of the men pointed for me to look. Packy and I walked between them and got our first view of the hidden valley. It was special, that first seeing. I could tell that Packy liked the looks of it, too, by the way she was holding her head.

The valley was more than a mile across and several miles long, surrounded by jagged hills. There were about fourteen lodges on the valley floor. Off toward the left a split-rail corral held a dozen horses. At the far end was a dense pine forest. Several cook fires were sending up smoke. Small children were running around the set-tlement playing some sort of chase game. A creek snaked through the center.

Shanti was at my side. *"Wallama,"* he said. It looked like a welcome place.

We picked our way down the hill and walked our

horses toward the village as the sun set over to our left. I didn't want to look scared. Several people came out of their lodges to watch us approach, and all of them looked me over pretty good, especially the kids. The kids looked curious and a bit frightened. Everybody else just looked.

Shanti held the shoulders of an older man. They said a few words. He put his arm around a woman and said something to her that made her smile, then he turned to me and motioned for me to get down.

We began to get acquainted. Three other men had walked over, and Shanti went through them one at a time, telling me about them, telling them about me. I didn't get any of it, but it seemed to go all right. Each of the men looked me in the eye while Shanti talked. I looked back at them. When Shanti was through, they would nod their heads and I nodded back. Big Nose took Packy's reins and pointed toward the corral. I let him have her, but Packy bolted and pranced until I gave her a pat and told her it was okay.

One man stood off from the rest. Something was wrong with him. He was never still, his face would twitch and jerk, then his arms and hands while his mouth twisted and eyes rolled. I didn't stare at him.

Shanti motioned for me to follow him and bent over to push through the doorway of a lodge. It was dark with a small fire burning inside a circle of rocks. The smoke rose through a hole in the roof. The floor was hard-packed dirt. Around the walls were layers of furs and pelts laid out on a ledge.

There was a young girl nursing a baby. She glanced up at me, then back down at her baby and watched it with a sweet look on her face. It was the exact same look my mom used to have when she nursed my little sister.

She hummed and rocked as it sucked away. Shanti talked with his father while his mother fussed around the fire. I wanted to watch the baby, but I was afraid the girl would think I was just trying to peek at her titty. I watched smoke curl through the hole in the roof and rocked back on my heels.

Shanti's mom handed me a clay cup filled with hot, steaming liquid. She never looked up at me. I said, "Thank you." She gave Shanti and his dad cups, and they wrinkled their faces as they drank. I took a sip. It was bitter and sweet at the same time and not very good. I drank some more anyway. They looked at me and I nodded and smiled: "Delicious."

Shanti's mom poured some flour meal into a clay bowl of water and stirred. She used two sticks to pinch up some hot rocks from the fire and dropped them into the bowl. Shanti said, *"Pocka, pocka,"* and pretty soon that is the sound that the water made as the stuff cooked. *Pocka, pocka.*

Shanti, his father, and I sat around the bowl and ate the gruel. They used their first two fingers like spoons, so I did too. It was bitter and made my teeth feel sharp, but filled me up. Shanti called it yuna, and it might have been acorn meal. Some honey would have helped it. Or sugar.

Big Nose came in and sat next to the young girl. She had finished nursing the baby, and Big Nose pulled back the blanket to look at it. He smiled and bobbed his Adam's apple up and down. He made little sounds to it for a while, then sat down next to us and ate some of the yuna mush. He seemed to like it. The men kept up a conversation back and forth. I tried to listen to the words carefully. They never made an *r* sound, and once in a while made a clicking noise with their tongues. I guess my talk sounded funny to them too.

After we ate, Shanti and his dad sat on the ledge of furs, leaning back against the wall. Big Nose went over and took the baby from the young girl, and she and Shanti's mom ate from the bowl. Big Nose rocked the baby and talked to it softly. I walked over to him and bent down to look at his child. Big Nose pulled the blanket from its face. I was glad to see that it had a regular-sized nose. The baby was beautiful and I said so. Big Nose smiled up at me and pulled the blankets away to show me the baby's privates. It was a boy. Big Nose pointed and said, "Huh, huh?"

I said, "Yeah, there it is."

A young boy of ten or so came through the doorway and said some words to Shanti's dad. He was excited and looked at me with his eyebrows up. Shanti's dad took a deep breath and stood up. He said some words to me in a serious voice. I wished I knew what they meant. I followed him and Shanti outside into the darkness.

◆ 14 ◆

Nobody had to tell me that he was the chief. He didn't have on a big feather hat or special clothes, just fur robes over his shoulders. He had eagle eyes and face wrinkles. They were more like weather wrinkles than old wrinkles.

His lodge was about like Shanti's, a little bigger and with log benches on two sides of the fire. A skinny Indian wearing a suit coat and dress hat sat across the fire from me. He said, *"¿Su hablo mexicano?"*

"Sí," I said. *"Un poco."* That meant, "A little." Two years ago a Mexican man had spent the winter with us. Antonio and I would sit around and teach each other words from our own languages. *"Palabras,"* he called them. I learned a lot of Mexican talk that winter but didn't know how much I remembered.

I pointed to the chief. *"Esto el hombre número uno?"*

"Sí." The skinny Indian smiled. *"Majapa, el jefe."*

I nodded. The Indian with all the twiches and jerks was standing back in a corner, half in shadow. He made me edgy.

The skinny man knew a few words of English, a lot of Mexican, and his people's tongue. It took a long time and a lot of back and forth, but we managed to have good talk. They wanted to know how I knew where to come to look for Shanti.

I told them the best I could about letting the arrow-head necklace swing and point me the way. I took it off, held it by the thong, and showed them. Even sitting in the lodge, it swung toward Shanti, and it seemed to work them up. I told them about the hawk that helped me find the way too.

I thought they might laugh, but they didn't. The chief seemed more interested in me than before. Shanti said some words, and the skinny Yani said, *"Amigos de la corazón"*—friends of the heart—and pointed to Shanti, then me.

I said, *"Sí."*

The chief told a story, and the skinny man told it to me in Mexican. It went something like, "God made a man out of dirt and put it in a hole with fire to cook. He did not cook it long enough, and when it came out, it was too white. Like you." He pointed at me.

"God made another man. This time he left it cook too long, and it came out burned and charred. *El negro*, the black man.

"God made another man, and this time cooked it to perfection. That was the Yahi."

I didn't know if this was supposed to be a joke or a serious story. The chief watched me closely as the story ended. His face looked stern at first, but I thought I saw the corners of his mouth turn up just a bit, so I took a chance and said, *"No, los hombres blancos es perfectos."*

The chief smiled, tapped my shoulder, and talked.

The skinny man said, *"El jefe* says Reece has words that laugh," in Mexican talk.

I learned that Shanti's father was The-man-who-keeps-the-legends-of-the-people and He-who-dreams-the-truth. Majapa was the main chief, and Big Nose was the war chief. It seemed like a pretty good way to split up the jobs. The skinny man had spent two seasons at a mission where the Mexican priests had told him about "The New Book of Heaven," *La Biblia*.

The jerking man had his back to us, facing a corner doing a little nervous dance. I wanted to ask about him, but figured they would get to it sooner or later.

Shanti's dad saw me looking and said, "Mechicuwi," and nodded toward the corner.

The skinny man said, *"Curandero demonio."*
Demon doctor? One who cures with demons?

Shanti's dad wanted to know the white man's story of the beginning of the world. I told him the story of creation from Genesis as best as I remembered. He pushed out his lips and nodded his head and then told me his ideas.

"The father of all fathers came inside himself and made the sun to look upon the mists and form the great salty waters. After much time the sun cooked out the green slime that rode on top of the water and swayed up and down, this way and that way. Much time passed, and little creatures began to swim and crawl in the slime. After more seasons the slime became the land, and the tiny creatures grew and had many forms."

Not bad. I pushed out my lips and nodded. I suppose everybody wonders about how the world got here and has their own stories about it.

Next Shanti's father told about his dream. It had something to do with a fox who was afraid of the moon, and I couldn't get any sense out of it. Everybody else acted like it was important stuff, so I frowned and nodded and pushed my lips out again.

Then I told about my dream. I'm sure it came out all

mixed up after my Mexican being turned into Yahi, but I took my time, and so did the skinny man. Shanti's dad came over to me and put his hand on the top of my head. He said that my dream was "the dream of one a little bit dead" or something like that.

A little bit dead? It seemed like a good thing to call that dream. I had thought about it over and over ever since that night, trying to figure it out and make some sense out of it. Maybe I had died a little bit. Or maybe I had just froze and thawed out. Those people in the dream had seemed so real, especially Dad.

A woman brought in bowls of that bitter-tasting tea, and we all sipped it and watched the fire burn. The skinny man told me, "There are memories in the fire."

I said "*Sí*" again. The tea made the back of my throat feel tight. I looked in the fire as if I saw some memories in there. It seemed like the polite thing to do.

The chief finished his tea and made a big yawn. I knew what that meant. Everybody stood up, and we made our way back to Shanti's lodge. Big Nose and his wife were lying together along the right wall. Shanti's mom was lying along the left. His father joined her, whispering softly. I heard her laugh quietly.

Shanti pointed to a place for me to lie, and I stretched out on my side. Shanti shook his head, made some sounds, and motioned for me to turn. I noticed that everyone else was lying with their heads toward the door, so I did too.

Skinny came in and stood over me. He told me, "In the tomorrow we will see the rocks of gold."

I said, "Okay, *sí, gracias,* thanks, *buenas noches,*" and fell asleep.

❖ 15 ❖

I dreamed all night of Kathryn.

She was with other men and they were nice to her and they didn't go upstairs, but still, she was with other men. She talked with them and they laughed together.

It was a foolish thing to feel the way I did for Kathryn after just one time together. Foolish or not, there it was. When Dad had lain there in his fever, he talked about women and what I should look for in a wife. "First thing," he said, "most important is you find a woman who laughs easy. Second, she likes to be held and will hold you back without you having to beg. And get you one that's honest, if you can. Looks don't mean a whole lot, they really don't. 'Course," he said, "they don't hurt anything either."

I could hear Kathryn's laugh as I lay in the darkness. I could feel her too. I wondered if she was awake, thinking of me.

I rolled on my side. Shanti's mom was squatted by the fire, her back to me. I could smell meat cooking. She turned and looked directly at me. It was too dark to see her face with her back to the fire, but I raised a hand to her, and after a moment she raised her hand back.

I crawled out from under the furs and felt for my boots. Big Nose was snoring from across the room. Next to me the pile of furs shifted and I heard, "Leece."

I whispered, "Shanti."

He sat up smiling and rubbed and scratched here and there before he stood and touched my shoulder. I followed him outside, and we walked into the pine woods. We stood with our backs to each other and passed water. Shanti said, "Augh," and so did I.

We ate some more of the yuna mush gruel stuff with some cooked meat and drank some of the bittersweet tea. It tasted better than it had the day before. Shanti's dad walked to the doorway and said, "Leece." I followed him out into the village grounds, and we walked together to the rail corral. Skinny was there. He told me, "We go to see the rocks of gold."

I got Packy saddled up, and the three of us rode west. There was a large lodge set off from the others. I asked Skinny about it, and he told me it was for women to live in for some days every month when they were *"enferme loco."* I think it meant, "Sick crazy." I nodded like I knew what that meant.

We climbed the hillside as the sun rose and warmed our backs. It was a fine morning with some high cotton clouds. As we reached the top of the hill, a dove made its song off to our right. I cupped my hands and blew into the hollow through my thumbs, doing my own dove call. I can do a dove well enough to call them in to me and wanted to show off. The dove answered, and Shanti's dad smiled and said some words.

Skinny turned to me. "This is the story of dove," he said. "Dove was playing. A friend came to him and told him his mother was dead. Dove said, 'I play now. Later I will be sad.' Dove has been sad ever since."

Pretty good story. The dove spoke again, and the song sounded even sadder than before. I wondered about how long they had been telling that story, father to son and father to son. And I wondered about who made it up in the first place.

We rode another hour, stopping once to drink from a small creek and again while Shanti's dad gathered some dry leaves and twigs, stuffing them into a leather pouch slung over his shoulder. We dismounted at the base of a steep hillside.

We left the horses and half climbed, half crawled up the slope. It was mostly rocks with a scrub tree here and there, clinging with slender roots in the shallow soil. Shanti's dad led the way. I followed Skinny and didn't look down.

They disappeared behind a fold in the rock. I followed, turning sideways to squeeze around a bend, then stooping to scuffle under an overhang. Skinny was on hands and knees, waiting. He pointed toward a round opening, said, *"Caverna,"* and crawled through. I followed.

After a few feet there was no light. I heard them talking up ahead and pushed on. I bumped up against Skinny, and he said, *"No movimiento."* I sat back on a dusty floor. It even smelled dark.

They spoke together softly and shuffled and scraped around. I heard a stick break. Then another. I took my clump of matches from my pocket and used a thumbnail to peel out a wooden match.

The matchlight played shadows around the walls. Shanti's dad and Skinny were hunched together a few feet away. They had a small pile of leaves and twigs, and Skinny was twirling a stick between his palms. He smiled and said, *"Fósfero."* I guess that meant "match." I crawled forward and lit the leaves and tinder.

Skinny spoke in Mexican. "White men bring two good things only, the matches and the pockets."

We added some sticks, and I looked around in the flickering firelight. The cave was ten feet wide or so and got narrower toward the back and ended in darkness. Skinny picked up a burning stick and walked toward the wall on the left.

The vein started at knee level and widened as it crept and curved up and to the right. It looked like a big fat yellow snake, ten feet long. There was no telling how deep it was, but I knew for sure that I was looking at enough gold to make a lot of people rich. I whispered, *"Mucho oro."*

Skinny whispered, *"Sí."*

"Mucho, mucho oro." I ran my fingers along the paystreak of gold ore. Some pieces had been chipped out. I pointed and said, *"Dónde está?"*

"Para los soldados de la fortaleza," Skinny said.

For the soldiers at the fort. No wonder they followed Shanti and his friends. Shanti's dad jabbed at the vein with a pick with a broken handle. He knocked off two pieces, picked them off the ground, and handed them to me. They were heavy and cool in my palm but felt warm when I slipped them in my pocket.

We left the cave and made our way down the cliff. The snow was beginning to melt under the steady sun. We mounted and rode east, back toward the valley. There was enough gold in my pocket to buy a whole winter's furs. Skinny said, *"El caverno de oro es secreto, por favor."*

I turned and looked back. *"Sí."* I thought about it. It would take me less than an hour to chip away enough gold to last a lifetime. The Indians wouldn't miss it. I said it again, *"Sí,"* and thought about it some more as we rode along.

"Always do what's right," Dad had said. I tried not to think about his words, but they kept sounding inside my head. I imagined me and Kathryn in some fancy restaurant back east. We would eat things like lobster and drink wine and live in a hotel and have lots of clothes and . . .

Shut up, Dad.

✦ 16 ✦

I told the chief by way of Skinny that the gold would buy much land for his people. There was a lot of talk back and forth before Skinny said, "Land cannot be owned. The land is there, like the air, the sun, the rain."

I said, "Maybe so, but the way of the white man is to buy land with money. The white men have paper that says the land is theirs."

After more talk with the chief, Skinny said, "The way of the white man is the wrong way."

I shrugged my shoulders. "Perhaps it is the wrong way, but it is the way it is and the way it will be. More white men are coming. The old ways are gone."

When Skinny told my words to Majapa, he hard looked me. He breathed in through his nose and pursed his mouth up real tiny and talked.

Skinny said, "Majapa say Reece is young boy, he has not many seasons. The people have had their ways forever. The words of a young boy cannot change the traditions of the fathers and the fathers of fathers."

The chief and Skinny were silent as I thought it over. It took me a while because I didn't want to make them mad. The crazy guy walked up to the fire, jerking his shoulders and twisting his face. I got my Mexican words lined up in my head before I spoke.

"My father was a man of many years and much wisdom. He read books that had the words and wisdom of men long dead." I waited while Skinny told Majapa what I had said.

I told them about Dad falling through the ice and how he took to bed with his fever and chills. "Dad knew that death was near," I said. "He talked to me every day, all day. He told me all the wisdom he had. I remember all his words. They were the words of a father who knew he would leave his son soon. He wanted to give me all that he knew. I have only a few years, but I speak the words of my father who had many years."

Skinny talked to the chief, and the chief talked back. Skinny said, "What did your father know of the ways of our people?"

I shook my head. "*Nada.* My father did not know of your ways. He talked about the ways of men and the ways of the world. He said that the ways of the world were hard. He said that the ways were not just, he said the ways were not the way they should be."

Skinny and the chief spoke while I figured out my next words. "My father said that the way of the world is the way of the world. The world does not care if men do not like its ways. The wishes of men are not important. Things are like they are. Things are not the way men want them to be."

Skinny gave my words to the chief, and the chief was silent for a minute before he spoke. "Majapa say that your father has good words that he must think about and dream about. He say that Reece has much wisdom to hear the words of his father. Majapa also hears the words of his father and his father's fathers. The words tell him to keep the old ways forever."

I got a real sad feeling, almost the same feeling I had the night before Dad died. I looked into the flames of the fire, and memories came in my head. I remembered sitting next to Dad and touching his cold forehead, holding his cold hand. "The ways of the world are not always fair," he had said.

I had dug his grave on top of a little hill that looked over our cabin. "Things are the way they are," Dad had told me. "They aren't the way we want them to be." I walked back to the cabin wanting Dad to be alive and waiting there for me. I picked him up in my arms and carried him up the hill, looking into his sweet face, so peaceful and still.

Packy followed me up the hill and stood rock still while I shoveled dirt over Dad. I stood with her and looked at the grave until the sun went down. I slept that night in the stable with Packy. I had pulled down some hay for her, but she wasn't hungry either. When spring came, I planted an apple seed over Dad's grave. The apple seedling is almost three feet tall now.

The fire popped and sent a spark flying. I found myself crying over the memory, sitting there across from the chief and Skinny. The jerking man bent over to look at my face. He reached out and touched a tear, then tasted it off his fingertip. He reached out for another tear, and I pushed his hand away.

Skinny said, "*¿Porqué lágrimas?*"

I think it meant, "Why tears?"

I said, "I have sad words to say. They are words from my father and from my heart." I began talking and the words came out. I don't know where they came from. At times I wanted to stop speaking, but the words just came on their own.

"The ways of the Yahi are fading. The white man's ways are growing. The white man speaks of many good things. He speaks words that say All Men Are Created Equal. He says that all men are brothers. He says that all men are children of the Great Chief in the Sky. He says that all men have the right to live and to keep what is theirs."

Skinny spoke with Majapa while I stared into the fire. When he quit talking, I said, "The white men say these words, but they do not hear them. The white man thinks that his ways are the only good ways. He believes that the ways of your people are not as good, are not the true ways. He does not think it is wrong to take from the Yahi and to lie to him."

While Skinny gave my words to Majapa, I watched the fire burn. "The Yahi people must learn to take the ways of the white man. The white men are many. They will come into the land of your people and take from them. They will bring guns and soldiers and make fences of wire."

I waited while they sorted out my words. Then the chief spoke, and Skinny turned to me and said, "The white man is one, the Yahi is one. The Father of Fathers gives the rain to the white man, the Yahi. He makes the sun to shine on the white man and the Yahi man. They are the same and not the same. They must live together and not together. We will tell the white man of the gold they desire, and they will leave us in peace."

I remembered playing cards with Dad and the Mexican man. We talked about cheating. He called it *"defraudado."* I looked at Majapa, *"Los hombres blancos defraudados los indios. Esto certemente."*

I think I said it right enough. "The white man will cheat the Indians. It is certain." Skinny talked to the chief. Then the chief talked with the jerky Indian for a while.

There was more Yahi talk before Skinny told me, "We go now." We left Majapa's lodge and walked toward the corral. I asked Skinny about the jerky man. *"Es loco?"*

"No, no," Skinny said quickly. He told me that he was the man who spirits of the dead lived inside. *"Espíritus de la muerte."* He told me that he was very *"importante."*

Packy was glad to see me and came over for some nose rub. The day had warmed under steady sun, and the snow was melting. Patches of earth were showing. Skinny pointed north toward the pine forest, where a plume of smoke was rising. "Shanti," he said. *"Forma la casa."*

Shanti build a house. I said, "We go?"

Skinny said, "You go."

Packy was glad to get her saddle on.

◆17◆

Shanti and his friends had several fires burning. They had worked up some clay and plastered it around the trunks of the trees like a thick collar, two feet off the ground. The fires were burning into the trunks, under the collars, and as the trees charred, they beat at the trunks with stone-headed clubs. The band of clay protected the rest of the trunk from the flames.

There were eight horses off to the side, each tied to scrub trees. I rode over and jumped down, letting Packy's reins hang. It would have hurt her feelings to be tied like the others.

They were all young men about Shanti's age. There was a lot of talk and laughing and shoving and punching as they went about the work. Shanti seemed to be in charge. I walked over to him, and we shook hands. Shanti had taken a strong liking to handshakes.

I made a bunch of gestures to let him know that I wanted to help, and he handed me a club and pointed to one of the tree fires. I joined another young fellow and began beating at the base of the trunk, knocking sparks and pieces of charred wood as the fire ate into the heartwood. It wasn't a job I'd want to have every day, beating a tree, but it felt good to be doing something useful.

About twenty feet away two braves had stopped pounding their tree and were looking up. The tree had begun to sway, and only a small section of trunk remained under the collar as if a giant beaver had chewed away at it. They pointed up and said a word, *"Mowka."* Two of them began pushing against the tree. There was a cracking sound, and they yelled that word again, *"Mowka."*

The tree rocked and leaned. We all stopped working and moved back. They pushed again, and the tree gave out a loud crack, leaned farther, groaned sadly from its center, then began to fall. It gathered speed and hit the earth with a crash that shook the ground under our feet.

The Indians' horses stomped and fought the reins. Packy stood quietly and watched. She has too much sense to get worked up over a tree falling down. The workers were all quiet as they walked over to the tree. They each touched the fallen pine and muttered some words to it. I don't know what they said, but they seemed real solemn. I walked over to the tree, patted the trunk, and said, "Sorry, tree."

They all stood around for a while, heads down, like mourners at a grave. Then Shanti said some soft words, and they all got back to work.

It took another hour to get our tree burned through. As it started to fall, I yelled *"Mowka"* with the others and joined them as they stood around the fallen pine, heads down and silent. They said quiet words and touched the tree farewell. I gave the trunk a pat and said, "Sorry, old fellow," as if I was serious about it.

Shanti took six paces and marked the trunk. They got another clay collar wrapped at the mark and started a small fire under it. Shanti checked the sun, low over the western mountain range that rimmed the valley. He pointed toward the village.

We mounted up. Shanti rode a big white stallion with faint dark circle marks along its back and sides. One eye was enclosed with a perfect ring of black. As we rode toward the lodges, the stallion acted skittish. He would bump against Packy and nip at her neck. Shanti spoke to him, jerked at the reins, and kicked the stallion's sides with his heels.

Packy was acting up, too, tossing her head and turning away from the stallion. I had never kicked at her and wasn't about to start. I figured she had her own good reasons.

The others had turned their horses into the corral and were standing by the gate, watching us as we rode our lunging mounts toward them. They laughed and pointed, mostly at Shanti, who was having a worse time than me.

Skinny came trotting over and grabbed the stallion's reins near its mouth and spoke harshly. The stallion didn't take to that and reared up, jerking Skinny up in the air. He hung on, one-handed, kicking his legs.

Two more braves had to help before they got the horse corralled with the others. Even then the stallion tried to squeeze past through the gate before they got it shut. It stayed by the gate and nickered at Packy, and she did a little dance about that and whinnied back at him.

Shanti said "Leece" from behind me. He was standing in back of Packy with Skinny. He motioned to me, and I jumped down. Shanty raised Packy's tail and pointed at her rear end. The skinny Indian said, *"Su caballo es en celo."*

I was pretty sure that *celo* meant "hot." *Your horse is in hot?* I said, "What?"

Skinny said, *"Crianza."*

I shook my head. *"No comprende."*

Packy didn't like it, them looking at her private parts. I took Shanti's hand away so her tail hung down like it was supposed to.

Shanti made a circle with his left thumb and forefinger. He stuck his right forefinger in the circle and pushed in and out a few times. Then he pointed to his stallion, then Packy. I was beginning to grab hold of their meaning. Skinny said, *"Será una buena madre."*

Packy had walked over to the corral. She and the stallion stood with their necks together. I went over to them, and Packy turned her head for a nose rub, then turned back to the stallion. She had never turned away from a nose rub before, so I knew the stallion must have been pulling on her pretty strong. I said, *"Sí,* okay," and made that same gesture with my fingers that Shanti had. It was kind of embarrassing.

Shanti opened the gate, and the stallion came prancing out, tossing his head and holding his tail stiffly raised. He and Packy touched noses, then trotted off, side by side. They wanted some privacy. I yelled, "You be nice to her, hear?" and watched them until they were out of sight across the valley.

~18~

We ate boiled meat mixed in with pale yellow roots that tasted something like turnips. I said, *"Mucho gusto,"* to Skinny, and he told Shanti's mom, and she grinned with her head down.

I told Shanti and his dad through Skinny about how I had to return to Macland to talk to the judge. Skinny must have known something about white men's law because he talked a long time and answered questions that Shanti's dad was asking. I told them how I would have to run away forever unless Shanti would come with me and tell the truth to the judge.

There was a lot of talk between them. Big Nose was making his baby laugh by making faces at it. It was a sweet sound, like music and birds and running water. I wanted to get in on it, but was afraid that I'd make the baby cry with my white man's faces. Big Nose's wife thought it was funny too. She had a space between her top front teeth and covered her mouth when she laughed.

They talked a long time, leaving me out of it. After a while Big Nose handed his baby back to his wife and stood up. He stretched and yawned, then walked toward the doorway. He bent to go through, then turned to wave at me, and I got up and followed him.

It was a fine, cold, clear night. We walked to the stream and drank. The water made my teeth hurt. Big Nose looked up at the sky and pointed to some stars. He said, "*Montok teck.*" I said, "Big Dipper," and he nodded. We walked away from the village and he told me the names of various stars and star bunches. He had stories to go with the names, and they were probably good ones.

When we got back inside the lodge they were still talking it over. Big Nose looked at his sleeping baby while I listened. He came over to the fire and pointed for me to sit down. He sat down facing me and handed me four teeth. They might have been from a wolf, but I couldn't be sure. He had four teeth in his hand that he placed on the dirt floor in a square. He pointed to the teeth in my hand and made sounds.

I didn't know what to do, so I put my teeth down in a square, too, and Big Nose nodded yes. He moved his teeth around to form a straight line, and I did the same with mine. It seemed to please him. He picked up a flat rock and stood it on edge to hide his teeth as he moved them around. He pointed to me and grunted.

It seemed like a pretty dumb game, but I shifted the teeth around on the floor, and Big Nose moved his rock so that I could see. He shook his head no and raised the rock again. After a while I began to catch on to the game. There was a large tooth, two middle-sized teeth, and a small one. I was supposed to try to guess how he had arranged the ones on his side of the rock and fix mine the same way. I came real close one time, and Big Nose pushed the flat rock toward me.

My turn. I shuffled the teeth around behind the rock.

Big Nose made a very serious thing about it, first looking into my eyes and making a little humming sound from deep in his chest.

He missed. I moved the teeth, and he took another try and this time guessed perfectly. It made him happy. He turned and talked to the others, and they came over to see for themselves.

Big Nose went next and made his moves behind the rock and looked up. I did the look-into-his-eyes thing and began moving my teeth around in the dirt.

Shanti was standing close to me and was tapping my behind with the side of his foot. It was a signal. I would move a tooth from place to place until he tapped, then move around another tooth until he tapped again. When he gave me three quick taps, I figured that meant I had it right. He was standing toward my side and could see both sides of the rock. I crossed my arms over my chest and nodded.

They made a big fuss over me getting it right. We did it again, then again, and there was even a bigger fuss. After the fourth time Big Nose threw up his hands and stood up.

The skinny man took his place and moved the teeth around out of my sight, behind the rock. I got it right with my teeth, thanks to Shanti's foot-tap signals. Skinny got very worked up about it. He slid the teeth around again, mumbling to himself. I got it right again, acting serious about first looking into his eyes before moving a tooth. The hard part was to keep from laughing about the way they were carrying on.

"*Es fácil,*" I said. That meant, "It's easy."

Skinny took another try. He had sweat on his face and chewed at his bottom lip. After he got the teeth in place, he closed his eyes and covered them with his palms.

"*No justo,*" I said. "Not fair." He kept his eyes covered and said, "*Movimiento dientes.*"

I said, "*No es posible,*" and shook my head. I think I did a pretty good acting job. I shut my eyes and rubbed my temples for a while. It was very quiet in the lodge. I kept my eyes closed and reached for a tooth, moving it slowly, this way and that, until Shanti tapped my behind. I put it down, took a deep breath, and picked up another tooth. I moved it around until he tapped again. After I got all four teeth placed, Shanti gave me three quick taps. I said, "*Finito.*"

Skinny took a look. His eyes got very big. He jumped to his feet and pointed at the teeth, speaking very fast in Yahi talk. Shanti's dad and Big Nose were excited too. Big Nose wanted to try the teeth game again, but I said, "*No más,*" and scooted backward, toward the fire. Sooner or later they would have caught onto us.

Shanti's mom passed out some of that tea again. Shanti sat on the ledge, leaned back, and sipped. He gave me a sneaky grin, and I eye-winked at him. The other three men talked back and forth. Shanti's mom stood close to me and tapped me with the side of her foot, just like Shanti had, but she never said a word.

I joined Shanti on the fur-covered ledge. After a while Skinny came over, pointed to Shanti and me and said, "*Vamanos Macland por la mañana.*"

We go to Macland in the morning.

-19-

We had yuna gruel again in the morning. I was getting used to it, but it still tasted like yuna.

Big Nose had ridden off and brought back our horses. Packy looked a whole lot different. While Shanti said good-bye to his parents, I got her saddle on and her nose rubbed. The stallion stayed at her side, so I did his nose with my other hand. He looked kind of different, too, all mellowed down from yesterday.

It looked like the whole Yahi village had come out to tell Shanti good-bye. The men came to the front and said words to Shanti and to me. The women stood farther back, and I watched Shanti glance at one over and over. The girl who smiled back was a real beauty. She had long hair done in two braids that fell down her front.

The chief came out of his lodge last of all. He spoke some words to Shanti, and Shanti tried to act like he was listening, but he wasn't. He had his mind on that pretty girl, and I didn't blame him.

Majapa looked over Shanti's shoulder and spoke to me. Skinny was at my side and told me that Majapa said that this was my home. All I could think of to say was, "Thank you, Majapa."

We walked our horses south, staying alongside the creek. I just happened to be looking at the crazy man's lodge when he came out his door and picked up an armload of firewood. He moved like a normal person, but when he turned to start back, he saw us and started the jerking and twitching business. I looked at Shanti. He hadn't seen what I had, and I wondered if I should tell him.

We climbed the hill. When we reached the top, Shanti turned to look back down into the valley. He had a special look on his face and didn't blink for a long time. I grunted and made motions with my hands that suggested long hair and breasts. Shanty nodded and looked back at the village. "Mondala," he said.

We picked our way down the steep slope, past the spring hole, and through the stream. We talked as we rode and taught each other words, such as *tree* and *rock*, and *mountain* and *snow*, and on and on. We said the words back and forth. "*Siwini*," I said.

"Tree," said Shanti.

"*Siwini*."

"Tree."

After a couple hours we passed the place where Shanti and his men had waited and rescued me from the sheriff. The day was warming slowly, and more snow was melting.

Shanti led the way. He kept a pace that put miles behind us without wearing down the horses. Now and then he would point and say some words, telling me about things that had happened, sharing his memories. A few times he stopped, and we sat together and enjoyed good scenery. He liked to look at the same kind of views I did.

We pushed along in a south-southeast direction. Toward midday we stopped to water our horses. In an area of open, sandy dirt I brushed away some sticks and began drawing. I scratched an *X* with my finger, pointed at Shanti, and put my wrists together like they were tied. He nodded. I pulled my knife and made cutting motions, like I was cutting the ropes they had tied his hands with. He understood.

I scratched a line in the dirt, showing my route into Macland, and drew a row of houses. "Macland," I said.

Shanti said, "Macland."

I handed him the knife, and he began a line northward toward his home village. He said, *"Wallama,"* and made a circle. I nodded.

I drew a house in the dirt, pointed to myself, and said, "Reece *wallama.*" I pointed to the ground we were standing on, then to our scratched-out map. "Where are we?" I asked. *"Dónde?"*

Shanti made an *X* about halfway between his valley home and my cabin drawing. He turned to look at the sun, then looked back down at our map. He pointed to the sun with his left hand and scratched the dirt with the knife in his right hand. As he lowered his pointing finger to show the path of the sun, he traced the route to my cabin with the knife point. The knife got to the cabin just as the sun set.

We didn't spend any see time, and Shanti pushed our horses a little harder as the sun tracked west. I was getting hungry toward late in the day and didn't recognize any landmarks. About the time I was thinking of looking for a place to make camp, I spotted a line of cottonwoods that touched a memory.

Shanti had dead reckoned pretty much on course. I whistled at him, and he turned around. I pointed up ahead to the right and took the lead. After another mile Packy got a sense of place and broke into a canter. Shanti rode at my side, and I pointed out some places and told him stories about things Dad and I had done. As the sun was setting behind the trees, I let Packy have her head. She got us home at last light.

◄20►

The stallion balked at the stable door, refusing to follow us into darkness. I got Packy unsaddled and pulled some hay down while Shanti wrestled around with his mount. We tried doing it together, Shanti pulling at the reins while I pushed his big rump, but he wasn't having any of that spooky-looking doorway. Shanti spoke to him and said his name, Asham, softly at first, then he yelled and slapped the stallion's sides. That didn't work either.

Shanti handed me the reins and picked up a stick. While I pulled toward the doorway, he gave Asham some licks on the hindquarters. The stallion backed even farther away from the door, and I couldn't stop him.

Shanti caught me smiling and didn't smile back. He frowned instead and said some rough-sounding words, found a bigger stick, and went to whacking his horse again. He grunted and took harder swings and looked at me in between. Asham reared up and snorted.

I said, "That's too hard, Shanti," and moved between him and the stallion. Shanti pushed at me, and I pushed him back. He pushed harder the next time, so I did too. The veins in his neck stood out. He took the stick back like he was going to hit me with it. I dropped the reins and got ready to go at it with him, when Packy came to the doorway and made some nickering sounds. I don't know who she was nickering at, but the stallion went trotting right on in.

Shanti and I stood our places, staring each other down. I could feel my blood beating hot. After a moment Shanti made some motions and spoke some words. I think it meant, "It is my horse. I will beat it if I want to."

I said, "Not with me around you don't."

He said, "*Saldu*," and turned his mouth down like it was a bad word.

I said, "Dirty dog," and showed him my teeth. I felt like I wanted to fight. I was scared at the same time.

We stood there, glaring at each other for a long time. After a while I started feeling kind of silly about it. If a stranger would have rode up right then, it would have been hard to explain what we were doing.

I could hear Packy and Asham nicker inside the shed. Maybe they were laughing at us. Shanti's mouth twitched a little, and for just a second he looked away. I let myself blink a couple times and dropped my shoulders. He gave a little nod.

I nodded back and said, "Come on," and turned. Shanti followed me inside. I pulled down some more hay, handed him two water buckets, and pointed toward the creek. He nodded and walked down the hill. I busied myself in our cabin, lit the kerosene lantern, and got the fire going in the wood stove. I arranged the chairs and went out to the stable.

Shanti was watching our horses drink. They stood side by side in the stall, like a couple of barroom buddies. I watched along with him for a while, then motioned for him to come inside with me.

There might come a time when I would have to fight with Shanti about something, and it was terrible to think about. It would be bad and end up with both of us beat up and hurt, and things would never be the same.

Shanti liked the cabin a lot. I had him sit in a chair while I went about cooking chores. He liked the chair a lot too. He would stand up and bend down to look at the underside of the seat, then sit back down. I said, "Chair."

Shanti answered, "Chaya."

I was short on supplies but made some sourdough biscuits to go with the beans and hen eggs. Shanti watched me with quick, dark eyes that saw everything. The cabin was warming, and I took off my parka and hung it on a wall peg. Shanti took off his fur robe and hung it on the next peg.

He held the spoon wrong and squeezed it too tight, but he liked it. We sat across from each other and ate and talked. Shanti said, "Leece, chaya." I nodded and pointed to his seat and said, "Shanti, chair."

He learned to say "table" and "eggs" and "beans" and let me know that he liked the food by making a rumble sound deep in his throat, licking his lips, and patting his belly. I said, "You're welcome."

After we washed the cook gear, I built up the fire some more and left the stove door open. I moved our chairs so that we could sit side by side and watch it burn while our food settled. I remembered the word he had said to me when he was angry and asked him about it. "*Saldu?*"

I didn't say the word just right because he repeated it back with a little different sound, "*Saldu.*"

"What's it mean, *saldu?*"

Shanti put his arm next to mine and pointed, first to

his forearm, then to mine. *"Saldu."* He took a pinch of my skin between his thumb and finger. *"Saldu."* He pinched up a bit of his own skin and said, "Yahi." I figured that *saldu* meant "white man."

He called the fire *"awna,"* and his name for my cabin was *"wowi."*

Shanti watched the fire and began talking. I stared into the flames as he spoke. His language had a songlike way to it, like some of the poems Dad and I used to read out loud to each other. His words felt at home and filled the room with a comfort. The bad feeling that we had when we almost fought had gone away, and we were friends again.

We talked for an hour or so. I put a big oak log in the stove and shut the door. I pointed to the bed, said, "Shanti, Reece," and closed my eyes. He was in favor of it. I took off my boots and stripped down to my long johns. Shanti took off his moccasins and leg wraps.

I pulled back the covers and pointed. Shanti frowned and glanced from the bed to the door. I remembered how they had slept inside his lodge, heads all toward the door. I pulled the foot of the bed away from the wall, slanting it toward the door, and swapped ends with the pillows and blankets. He smiled about that.

We climbed under the covers. I turned onto my left side and said, "Good night, Shanti."

"Poyo nan, Leece."

I lay there and stared into the darkness and started thinking of Kathryn again. I felt strong about her. When I closed my eyes, I could see her when she looked up at me, so small and pretty. She stepped toward me and then disappeared. The moan that came out of me was a surprise. I hadn't felt it coming.

I turned on my back and tried to think of nothing.

Thinking about nothing is hard because my mind keeps jumping around. Dad used to say that the only thing we could really control was our own mind. I wasn't very good at it.

Sometimes I could get my mind quieted down by just watching my breathing, paying attention to the air coming in, going out, like it was something going on apart from the me part of me. I got it going pretty good when Shanti moaned from beside me. I turned to look at him. There was just enough light to see glint from his open eyes looking back at me. He said, "Mondala."

I said, "Kathryn."

In the morning I walked up to Dad's grave under the apple tree. I took off my hat and stood there for a while and thought about him.

Shanti and I rode south. Around midday we came to the place where they were going to lynch him. It had only been six days ago, but it seemed much, much longer. We sat our horses and looked down on the memory for a few minutes, then rode on.

We kept our horses at a walk. I had been thinking things over and figured our best plan was to slip into Macland after dark. Shanti had shown a lot of trust in me, riding to a white man's town. I wondered if he was as scared as I had been riding into his *wallama*. He didn't act like he was worried about it, but it put a new kind of worry on me. Now I had somebody else to take care of instead of just myself.

When we came to the creek where we had traded gifts, I turned Packy to follow the creek downstream. We were still going in the general direction of Macland. It was longer this way, but I wanted to stay off the road, and we had several hours before sundown.

The creek spilled over a flat rock ledge, making a little one-foot waterfall into a deeper pool. It made a gurgle sound, like the voices of women laughing and talking in the distance. I jumped down and lifted out a pot and what was left of a sack of beans. I laid some rocks for a cooking fire and Shanti brought over some sticks.

I got the water boiling, added all the beans, and put on the lid. "We'll wait here," I said. I pointed toward the sun and slowly pointed down. "After sundown Shanti and Reece ride into Macland. Find Mr. Fitsimmons."

Shanti nodded. He looked at the pot, frowned, and rubbed his belly.

"Yeah, I know, Shanti. That's all there is."

Shanti stacked up some flat rocks near the fire. "Leece, chaya," he said.

"Thanks." I sat down. Shanti walked over to the pool edge, stared into the water for a while, then began taking off his clothes. I said, "What are you doing?"

Shanti pointed to the water, waved his arm and wrist like a fish swimming, and pointed to his mouth.

I said, "It's too cold, Shanti." I hugged my shoulders and shivered.

He nodded, smiled, and stepped into the tail of the pool. As he eased into deeper water he made a high-pitched sound, like a pig squeal. He made his way slowly toward the little waterfall, the water rising up to his belly. When he got to the falls, he stooped down and reached under the ledge.

It made me cold to watch him. I added some wood to the fire. Shanti worked his way across the waterfall. Toward the center he stopped, reached back farther, and ducked his head under. A moment later his head popped up. He yelled, "Leece," and heaved a nice-sized fish out of the water. He threw it toward me, and it hit the ground and flopped a foot in the air.

Shanti grabbed another fish toward the far end of the falls. It was a heavier fish, which thrashed and fought on top water. Shanti had his hand inside the gill cover. The fish went wild, jerked Shanti off his feet, and he crashed into the pool, came up spitting water, then went under again.

The next time he came up he was near the bank, and I was waiting for him. He grunted and lifted the fish toward me. I got down on my belly and grabbed his lower jaw with one hand, and we had him on the bank.

Shanti warmed himself at the fire while I gutted the small fish and cut steaks off the large one. Shanti was pleased with himself, and I was proud of him too. We would eat well. I bragged on his bravery and strength while I did the knife work and he smiled and shivered.

We used forked sticks to hold the fish over the fire, off to the side away from the main flames. Shanti got back into his clothes and gathered more firewood while I tended the food. When he got the fire fed, he sat beside me. I lifted the pot and watched the beans slow-boil. I said, *"Pocka pocka."*

Shanti agreed, *"Pocka pocka."*

We sat shoulder to shoulder and ate beans direct from the pot. Shanti was better with the spoon. We broke off flakes of steaming fish with our fingers, gave them a blow, and chewed slowly. We made a lot of sounds back and forth to each other, like "ummm" and "ahh." The small fish tasted better than the big fish, but we ate everything but the sticks.

Some buzzards were circling in the air downstream from us where the fish guts were drifting. We sat together and enjoyed the fire with full bellies while the sun dropped lower.

A dove made its song at last light and I answered it, blowing through cupped hands and remembering "the story of dove" that Shanti's dad had told. Shanti smiled in a sleepy way. It always made me sleepy to get real cold too.

When it started to get dark, I said, "Let's go to Macland."

Shanti said, "Macland."

✦ 21 ✦

From where we sat our horses we could look down on the whole town, stained in moonlight. Macland had grown a lot since I first saw it three years ago. I watched Shanti's face as he took it all in. I said, "Macland," and he said it back to me.

I pointed out the places of business, starting from the left. "That's the back of the livery," I said. "Then the blacksmith, Fitsimmons's trading post, Macland Bank, Lizzy's saloon, and the gunsmith. On the other side is the general store, the post office, a barber, the jail, Macland Hotel, the assayer and land office, and the restaurant." The sign over the restaurant said EAT.

I led the way, and Packy picked her way down the hillside. Fitsimmons's store was dark, but a light showed upstairs where he lived with his wife, Cora. The horses waded through the creek, the same one Shanti had wrestled the fish out of earlier. As we neared the back of Fitsimmons's stable, I could hear loud talk from Lizzy's saloon. A woman laughed. It wasn't Kathryn, but I knew she was over there.

I slid the latch and led Packy through the stable door. Asham walked through behind us without a fuss. I think he would have followed Packy off a cliff. We got the horses settled in and stood in the doorway, listening. It was the warmest night of the year so far and had that springtime feel to it. Some dogs barked back and forth from down the street.

Shanti followed me up the back stairs. I tapped the door with my knuckles, and Fitsimmons's voice said, "Who's there?"

"It's me, Reece, and I've got my friend with me."

Quick footsteps from inside, then the door swung open and Mr. Fitsimmons was grinning real big. He waved with his arm, "Come on in, son. Bring your friend."

I pushed Shanti on through first. Mr. Fitsimmons grabbed me by the shoulders and gave me a little shake before he took a quick look outside and closed the door.

Cora Fitsimmons was sitting beside the cook stove in a straight chair. She looked worse than last year. She said, "Come here, Herbert, and just let me look at you."

I took off my hat. "How are you, Mrs. Fitsimmons?"

"Look at you, getting so handsome." She reached out her hands, and I held them easy. Her wrists looked like there were rocks under the skin. "You look more and more like your father, God rest his soul."

"Thank you."

"Sit down, boys." Mr. Fitsimmons hitched his suspenders over his shoulders and pulled two chairs out from a table. I motioned to Shanti to come over. "This is my friend, Shanti," I said. "Shanti, this is Mr. Fitsimmons and his wife, Cora Fitsimmons."

They nodded and smiled around. Mr. Fitsimmons said, "You boys take a seat while I finish the missus's hair."

I looked at Shanti and pointed to the other chair.

Mr. Fitsimmons stood behind his wife and combed out a long, flat band of her yellow-gray hair and held it with his fingers. Then he wrapped it around an iron and held it there.

"Your horses in the stable?" he asked.

I said, "Yes, sir."

Shanti said, "Macland chaya."

I said, "That's right." I pointed to my seat and said, "Reece chair," and he smiled, pleased with himself.

Mr. Fitsimmons said, "Judge is due in the first of the month. That'll be about four, five days." He combed out another bunch of hair. "What day is this, Cora?"

Mrs. Fitsimmons said, "March twenty-eighth."

Shanti pointed and said, "Macland table."

I said, "Are Little Sam and Colby around?"

Mr. Fitsimmons rolled another curl. "Little Sam is. Ain't seen Colby for a few days."

Shanti said, "Fismon chaya."

I asked, "Have you talked to Kathryn any? I mean, you know, have you talked to her or spoken to her or . . . ?"

Mr. Fitsimmons said, "I'll go over later, tell her you're back. I better go talk with Sheriff Ames too." He gathered up another bunch of hairs and ran a comb through. He had big, rough hands, but used them in a gentle manner.

Shanti said, "Packy, Asham," and did that thing with his hands, making a circle with his thumb and forefinger and running his index finger in and out.

Mr. Fitsimmons said, "Hey there, watch that."

I said, "I'm sorry," and reached over to press Shanti's hands down. Mrs. Fitsimmons had her head lowered and was biting her lip. After a moment her shoulders started to shake.

"Tell that boy mind his manners," Mr. Fitsimmons said. "Doing that kind of thing around a lady."

"Oh, don't be such a stiff neck," Mrs. Fitsimmons said. "He's just trying to be part of the conversation. I thought it was cute."

"Well, I dunno."

Mrs. Fitsimmons looked at Shanti and smiled. "So, you're breeding your horses, is that right?" She raised her hands and did the same gesture that Shanti had done. It surprised me.

Mr. Fitsimmons said, "Cora, for God's sake."

Shanti got up from his chair. He stepped to Mrs. Fitsimmons and took her hands, touching here and there at her twisted fingers, her knotted joints. He frowned and mumbled to himself, then dropped to his knees and pulled up the hem of her dress. Her ankles were swollen and red too. He looked up at her and said, *"Solta met."*

Mrs. Fitsimmons said, "We call it arthuritis, Shanti."

Shanti said, *"Solta met,"* and lifted her dress to above her knees.

Mr. Fitsimmons said, "Hey! What the hell . . ."

Her knees looked awful. Shanti twisted up his face like he was feeling pain. He put his palms on each side of her left knee, then her right knee. He said it again, *"Solta met,"* very quietly.

Mr. Fitsimmons said, "Tell him quit fooling around my wife's legs, Reece."

"It's all right, Henry. His hands feel nice."

"Don't you let him go up no higher, Cora."

"Hush."

"And don't be taking no enjoys from it neither."

Mrs. Fitsimmons bumped her husband's leg with her elbow. "You're being silly, you old fool. Finish doing my hair."

Fitsimmons gathered up a few loose hairs and combed through them, mumbling to himself. Shanti held his palms on each side of Mrs. Fitsimmons's knee. After a moment he took his hands away and shook them down like he was whipping water off his fingertips. Then he held the other knee.

Fitsimmons took away the curling iron and patted around on his wife's hair. He held up a mirror for her, and she said, "That's very nice, Henry. Thank you."

Mr. Fitsimmons put away the hair tools and watched Shanti shake out his hands again. "How long's he gonna stay at that, Reece?"

"I don't know."

"We oughta go see Ames. You and me."

"Now?"

Fitsimmons nodded. "You think we leave him here with Cora she'll be all right?"

"I'll be fine, Henry."

"You think that's helping any, what he's doing?"

"Well, it's not hurting anything. You two go ahead."

I followed Mr. Fitsimmons out the door and down the back steps. He turned to look back up at the door. "By God, you should have seen her, Reece."

"Who?"

"Cora, before she got down with this damn arthuritis. Sun never rose on a better woman, a better person." He lit a long cigar, took several short puffs, and studied the glowing tip. "A beautiful woman who didn't act like a beautiful woman. Know what I mean?"

"I think so."

He put a hand on my shoulder. "You know why she takes to you so much?"

"No, sir."

"We had a son, little baby boy. Sickly right from the

start, and he died just a few days old. She's always . . .
Cora's always, well, I think she looks at you and thinks
he'd be about your age now."

"Oh."

"Ever love somebody so much that it hurt, Reece?"

"I don't know. I guess so." We started toward the
stables. "I loved Dad a lot. Still do. Wasn't till he was
sick and all that I knew how much I loved him."

"I know what you mean." He opened the stable door
and lit the lantern. Packy and Asham were standing close
together in a back stall. "By God, that's a fine-looking
stallion. You give them some oats?"

"No. Just some hay, Mr. Fitsimmons."

"Let's us give them a little treat." He half filled two
buckets with oats from a barrel. I hand-fed Packy, dip-
ping out the oats so she could lip them from my palm.
Fitsimmons held his bucket up to Asham.

I said, "I love this lady. I guess it's not the same,
loving a horse and loving a woman, but I sure do love
her. She got us through that storm. I couldn't see two
feet and she took us right home."

"I 'spect she loves you, too, Reece." He put the
bucket on the ground and stroked the stallion's neck as
he ate. "These two ought to throw a fine colt."

Fitsimmons doused the light and closed the stable
door. We walked up the alleyway aside his trading post.
"Preacher came through here last year and talked about
how nice it was in heaven. Harps and singing and ever
thing. After meeting, I talked to him outside and asked
him if they was guitars and fiddles in heaven. He said,
'No, just harps.' I asked him about animals. Asked him if
I'd get to see my dog again in heaven. Had this dog
when I was a kid. Best friend you could have. I asked him
if they was dogs up there."

"What did he say?"

"He said, 'No. Animals is not allowed.' So I says, 'Well, shit, preacher. I don't wanna go, then.' "

I laughed. "What did he say about that?"

"He said I could go to hell. Then and I told him he could go to hell too. How does he know what it's like, heaven?"

I said, "Did you ever watch squirrels playing in the woods?"

"Yep."

"They have a good time, looks like."

"I didn't ask him about no squirrels."

~22~

The sheriff's office was dark. Mr. Fitsimmons rattled the door and looked through the window through his cupped hands. He said, "I'll try the saloon."

"I'll go with you."

"No, Reece. Better nobody sees you. You just slip in them shadows around the side." He started to move off.

I said, "See if Kathryn . . ."

"Yeah, I know."

When Fitsimmons opened the saloon door, loud talk and hard laughter came through. I wondered why men liked saloons so much. Dad used to call it make-believe happiness.

Two men came out of the saloon. One was so happy that his friend had to help him walk. When they got to the corner of the building the happy man staggered to the side all bent over. I heard the sound of throwing up, a wretching gag, then the *plop, plop* sounds of vomit hitting the ground.

"Oh, Gawd," he said.

"Feel better, Harley?"

Harley didn't answer. He was puking again. It didn't sound like a good time. After a while they shuffled down the middle of the street. I heard Harley say, "I just wanta lay my head down somewheres."

Mr. Fitsimmons and Sheriff Ames came through the door and walked toward me. I stepped out of the shadows. The sheriff nodded at me and said, "Come on inside."

It was warm in the office. The sheriff slipped out of his coat, lit a lamp, and felt the coffeepot sitting on a potbellied stove. There was a door with a small barred opening in it. A voice came through, "Who's out there?"

The sheriff said, "Shut up." He poured coffee into three tin cups, placed them on a desk, and said, "Ain't got sugar."

He sat behind his desk and opened a black book. The coffee must have been sitting there a long time. The sheriff said, "So, you're giving yourself up here," he turned to look at a calendar hanging under a wall clock, "at nine P.M. on March the twenty-eighth."

"Yes, sir."

He wrote in the book. "How you spell Reece?"

"*R-e-e-c-e.*"

"First name?"

"Herbert. It's Herbert R. Reece."

The sheriff wrote some more, slammed the book shut, and said, "I'm taking a big chance here, Reece. You're charged with murder of a federal marshal. That's serious business, and there's two deputy marshals to witness against you."

Mr. Fitsimmons said, "Those two shit kickers—"

Sheriff Ames held up his palm. "I know. They don't smell right to me neither. That's why I'm going to let you walk out of here instead of locking you up with the horse thief."

The voice came through the door, "I didn't steal no horses."

"Shut up."

"They was give to me."

The sheriff said, "You got a dollar, Fitsimmons?"

"Yeah, sure."

"Bail is one dollar. I'm releasing you in Fitsimmons's custody, Reece. This is Thursday. You be here Monday, nine in the morning."

"Yes, sir."

"You bring that Shanti fella with you?"

"Yes, sir."

"He speak American?"

"Well, he speaks his kind of American."

"I'll get Dan there to help out."

Fitsimmons handed him a silver dollar. Sheriff Ames dropped it in the top drawer. "You two get out a here before somebody spots you." He stood up and turned down the lamp. "I gotta get back over to Lizzy's and bust some heads."

The voice from the back yelled, "And I was fixin' to give them horses back anyhow."

Sheriff Ames said, "Shut up."

We said good-bye on the street and headed for the trading post. Mr. Fitsimmons said, "Here" and held out his hand. He dropped three silver dollars into my palm.

"What's this for?"

"It's yours. Kathryn says it's yours. Says you forgot it."

"But I . . . this was for her."

Mr. Fitsimmons kept walking. I had to quick-step to catch up with him. "What else did she say?"

"Nothing."

"Did you tell her I was here, that I'd like to see her?"

"Yep. I told her all that."

"Well, what did she say?"

"She didn't . . . She just said give you that money."

"Well, did she—"

"Forget her, Reece."

"Why? I don't want to. I don't think I can forget her."

"Yeah, you can. You got to. Might's well start now."

We walked around the side of the building. Mr. Fitsimmons put one foot on his steps. He dropped his head and stepped back down. "Let's go check them horses."

I followed him back to the stables. He lit the lantern and sat it on a barrel. Packy and Asham were still standing side by side.

"Look at them two, Reece. I believe they had arms, they'd be holding one 'nother."

"Yeah." I rubbed Packy behind the ears. She likes it there the best.

Mr. Fitsimmons said, "She's with Little Sam, Reece."

"What do you mean?"

"She's with Little Sam, like I told you."

"Not . . . you mean she's sitting with him?"

"She's going upstairs with him, Reece. She's going upstairs with him regular."

"Well . . . aw damn."

He put his hand on my shoulder and I slapped it away, then felt sorry about it. I felt sorry about everything. Mr. Fitsimmons put his hand on me again, and I left it there. He said, "You want to take a poke at me or something?"

I shook my head. He kept his hand on me, and I rubbed Packy's ears some more. He gave my shoulder a couple pats. "Tell you what, son. I'm going up, see about

Cora and that Shanti fellow. You come on up when you want to."

"All right."

"And you take your time."

"Yeah."

"Want I should leave the light burning?"

"No."

I stroked Packy in the darkness, and she nuzzled my neck some. Nothing would ever be any good again.

I did a real good job in the darkness of Fitsimmons's stable, a good job of feeling sorry for myself. It was all right to let Packy in on it, but I was glad Fitsimmons had gone.

When Dad was lying in his fever bed, he had talked about times like this. "One of the worst things that can happen is when a friend does you dirty, son. It can work on you, make you turn crazy if you let it, eat away at your heart. But, you know what it means when that happens?"

"No."

"It means you was wrong. It means that you was wrong about thinking someone was your friend. Calling someone a friend don't make him one."

"I see."

Dad had one of his coughing fits. "When that happens you got to remember that it was *you* that was wrong. Don't go to pining away and beating yourself up about it. Everybody makes a mistake. All it means is that you made a mistake, you thought somebody was a friend and you turned out to be wrong. Made a mistake."

"Uh-huh."

"Then you just tell yourself, 'Well, I made a mistake,' and go right on about living your life. You haven't lost anything. You haven't even lost a friend. You just lost somebody you thought was a friend but found out different. Remember that, son. You can't lose something you never had in the first place."

"I see what you mean, Dad."

"And you got two ways at looking at things. One way is to think about all the things you don't have, the money you don't have, the friends you don't have and things like that. The other way is you can think about the things you do have."

Packy gave me a push and fluttered her lips. Good old Packy. I closed the stable door and made my way to the steps. I still had Packy, I still had Shanti as a friend, and the Fitsimmonses too. Halfway up I remembered I had a pocketful of gold and knew where there was a whole lot more.

I still wished I had Kathryn to go with it.

✦23✦

Mr. Fitsimmons's hands shook as he handled the chunks of gold. "You know what you got here, Reece? You got any idea what this is?"

"Yeah, it's gold."

"More'n that, son. My God, I know men spend their whole lives grubbing for gold and never find what you just took out your pocket." He turned the rocks and rubbed them with his fingertips. "If it's like you told it, you could tote your whole future out that cave in a saddlebag. Never have to work again, never have to worry about nothing."

"It's not mine. It belongs to Shanti and his people."

"Live anywhere you want, pretty women knocking at your door. Take your pick." He glanced across the room. His wife was lying on the bed. Shanti sat on the edge. He touched the side of her neck with one hand, her wrist with the other. She looked back at us. "It tingles, Henry. I can feel it."

Mr. Fitsimmons whispered, "What's he doing, Reece?"

"I don't know."

"Don't see how that can help her none, touch and feel around on her."

"He won't hurt her, Mr. Fitsimmons."

"You don't reckon he's taking pleasure feelings from it?"

"No, he's trying to help her. Shanti is a good person."

"How you know that?"

"I just know."

He handed the rocks back to me. "What you gonna do with this?"

"Shanti wants to buy land with it. Land for his people to have forever. That's why they went to the fort in the first place. They wanted to make peace and sign a treaty."

"They got yellow-dogged, didn't they?"

"I guess."

"They always do. Stinks, way we treat them."

Shanti stood up and walked around the bed. He sat on the other edge and placed his hands again, one at the side of Mrs. Fitsimmons's neck, the other on her wrist. She smiled at him and said something. Shanti mumbled back to her and she laughed.

Mr. Fitsimmons said, "What'd they say?"

"I couldn't hear."

"You think it was something dirty?"

"No."

He raised his voice, "You ain't gettin' worked up, are you Cora?"

"Hush."

Mr. Fitsimmons scratched the side of his neck. "They can't buy land, Reece. I just remembered."

"Why not? They have gold, lots of it."

He shook his head. "Gold don't do them no good. An Indian can't own land. Ain't legal."

"How do you know?"

"Old Dan, he saved up his soldiering pay and wanted a place for his family. They wouldn't allow it 'cause he was an Indian."

"Who wouldn't allow it?"

"Land Office. An Indian can't do nothing like that, legal things with documents, papers that you sign. A nigger can, or a Chinaman, but not an Indian."

I said, "That doesn't seem right."

"It ain't right. I didn't say it was right. When you think about it, they was the ones here first."

Shanti stood up. Cora Fitsimmons sat on the side of the bed moving her hands and arms. She smiled at us, then pressed her fists against the mattress and heaved up onto her feet. Mr. Fitsimmons started toward her. "Stay back, Henry," she said.

She steadied herself with a hand on Shanti's arm, then took a step, then another. She let go of Shanti and walked toward her husband. "Look at me, Henry. Just look."

"By God, Cora." They joined hands, and he stepped backward while she followed him. Shanti was smiling with his chest all stuck out.

"Sit down now, honey. Don't try to do too much." He led her to a chair, and Mrs. Fitsimmons dropped into it.

"It's wonderful," she said. "So wonderful not to hurt."

"Is it gone, the pain all gone?"

"Almost. Oh, it hurts a little bit, but nothing like the last few months."

Mr. Fitsimmons bent over and kissed the top of his

wife's head. He whispered something to her that made her laugh.

I said, "I think we ought to go, Shanti." I pointed to him, to myself, and then the door.

"Where you going, Reece?"

"Back to our cabin, I guess. Stay there till Monday."

"I wouldn't do that, son. Colby might be scouting for you."

"I'm not afraid of Colby, Mr. Fitsimmons."

"You oughta be. He's a backshooter, and if he comes, he won't be alone."

I thought about it. "We'll just lay out somewhere, then, for a few days."

Cora Fitsimmons said, "Stay here with us, Herbert. There's plenty of room."

"No, I wouldn't—"

"That's right, Cora. He wouldn't be safe here neither."

"Of course he would."

"You know how boys are. They like sleeping out anyway."

She gave him a look. I said, "We'll be fine, Mrs. Fitsimmons."

Mr. Fitsimmons patted her shoulder. "I'll be right back, Cora. I'll get them outfitted real good, then be right back."

We went down the rear steps. "You boys get saddled. I'm going around front, open the store. I'll get you some stuff to last you." He went down the alleyway at a trot.

We were waiting for him when he came through the stable door. He dropped two burlap bags and handed us each a rolled-up blanket. I lashed the blankets in back of my saddle. "Are you sure about Kathryn, Mr. Fitsimmons? You sure she's with Little Sam?"

"Yeah, I am, Reece. Wisht I wasn't."

I handed up a bag to Shanti, and he put it across his legs. I swung onto the saddle, and Mr. Fitsimmons handed up the other bag. It was heavy too.

Mr. Fitsimmons said, "Some good stuff there in them sacks. Couple hams, rice, beans, cook pots, plates. You ever eat canned peaches?"

"No."

"Two cans each. Wait'll you try them."

"Take it out of my fur money."

"No, Reece. This is . . . there's no charge."

"I can pay."

"No, you can't. This is from me. It's a present to Shanti for what he done, trying to help Cora."

"See you Monday, then."

"You boys come back Sunday night, after dark. Spend the night with us. They might be watching the trails Monday morning."

I clucked at Packy, and we moved off into the night.

◆ 24 ◆

We laid around and ate Mr. Fitsimmons's food for three days, and he sure was right about those canned peaches.

I used a stick to scratch pictures in the dirt. I would draw a deer and say, "Deer," and Shanti would say it back. Then he would tell me the Indian word, and I'd say that a few times. *"Banya."* We did the same thing with *horse* and *man* and *woman* and *tree* and *fish*, and on and on like that for hours at a time.

On Sunday morning I told him we would go back to Macland that night, pointing to the sun and swinging my arm to the west to show him the time. He nodded and said, *"Auxa." Auxa* meant "yes."

I took a walk to get some more firewood. When I came back, Shanti was busy at scratching around in the place we had cleared in the dirt. I dropped the sticks, and Shanti looked up. He said, "Cora Fismon," and pointed to the ground.

It sure did look like her. It was just her face and head, but I would have known it was her right off. He got the hair just right, piles of circles on top of her head, after the fashion. I smiled and said, *"Aiku sub,"* which meant something like "That is good."

While I cooked our ham and beans, he drew another picture. It was Mr. Fitsimmons this time, and it looked more like him than he did himself. I *aiku sub*bed some more.

We talked about this and that while we ate. I went down to the creek to wash out pots and pans. When I came back to the fire, Shanti pointed to the ground again.

It was a picture of the girl with braided hair falling in front of her shoulders. She was looking up and smiling. Even scratched in the dirt the picture had a warm feeling. "She is very beautiful, Shanti."

"Mondala," he said.

We lay down and watched the sun climb while our food settled in. After a while Shanti said, "Fismon man, Fismon woman, Reece woman?"

"No." Shanti looked at me. I thought about telling him about Kathryn and Little Sam. I could probably have made him understand that the little man who had whipped him was now with the woman I had thought might be my woman. It would have made him feel bad, and there was nothing he could do about it. One of us feeling bad was plenty.

When the sun got high I dropped off to sleep and had one of those crazy dreams that don't make any sense. When I woke up, Shanti was gone. So was Asham. I washed off in the creek, got a drink, and started some rice to cook.

Shanti rode in with a bundle of willow-tree branches —the long, slender ones that are like whips. He laid them down by my saddle and said, "Cora Fismon, *solta met.*"

I nodded and sliced off some ham. Shanti looked in the pot. "Ham, beans."

"Ham and rice," I said.

"Ham and lice."

He never could get the hang of saying *r*. Shanti made little *click* and *cluck* sounds when he talked in Yahi. When I tried to do the sounds, Shanti would laugh and shake his head, and I'd keep trying and keep getting it wrong. Sometimes I got it extra wrong on purpose because I liked to hear him laugh.

"Shanti eat ham," he said. It was his first sentence.

"Reece eat ham. Reece eat rice."

"Shanti eat lice."

"That's right."

He pointed at the fire and the pots, "Reece good eat Shanti."

I gave him a big *"Aiku sub,"* and Shanti said, "Thank you."

After we washed dishes, Shanti began taking off his clothes. He pointed to the pool, "Shanti water fish, Fismon woman, *solta met.*"

At sunset we rode toward Macland and stopped to watch the full moon rise. The moon was *wakara*, another good word that seemed to fit. We stood our horses and let the moonrise happen in silence. I was glad he was there to watch it with me.

Shanti had six fish in the burlap sack and the bundle of willow whips. Mr. Fitsimmons must have been watching for us, for he came in the stable as I was getting Packy unsaddled.

"Judge is here," he said. "Ames talked to him."

Shanti held out his hand for a shake and said, "Fismon."

"Hello, Shanti."

"Shanti water fish, Fismon woman eat, *solta met.*"

"What?"

"I think he wants your wife to eat fish," I said,

"She's better, Reece. Whatever it was Shanti did, she's better. Come on up and see her."

We followed Mr. Fitsimmons up his back stairs. Mrs. Fitsimmons was standing by the stove. Steam rose from two pots. She smiled as she wiped her hands on her apron and walked toward us slowly. "There's my two fine boys," she said.

She gave us both hugs. "Give them some coffee, Henry, while I fix supper."

We sat around the table. Mr. Fitsimmons said, "Colby's back. Saw him this morning. Talked to him."

"Is Kathryn still with Little Sam?"

"Yeah. They're pretty thick with one 'nother."

Shanti stood by Mrs. Fitsimmons. Mr. Fitsimmons said, "Colby said to give you a message. Said you give them what they want and you won't hang."

"I guess they want me to tell them where the gold is."

He nodded. "I reckon they do. You could tell them, Reece. Might be your best way out of this."

"I don't want to do that."

"I know you don't. Maybe you could tell them wrong. Tell them something, anything, so's they'd change their stories for the jury."

"We'll have a jury?"

"Yeah. Murder trial gets a jury 'cause it's so serious."

Shanti was doing a lot of talking with Mrs. Fitsimmons, and she was having trouble making it out. Shanti held a knife and squatted down to scratch a picture on the floor. I said, "Have you got a pencil, some paper?"

Mr. Fitsimmons fetched some paper and a short stub of pencil. I showed Shanti how to use the pencil and we sat down around the table. He drew quick pictures of a deer, a horse, and a pig. "Cora Fismon eat," he said, and shook his head no.

"He doesn't want you to eat meat," I said.

Shanti used both hands to draw, swapping the pencil back and forth. He seemed to be as good with one hand as the other. He made pictures of an apple, berries, beans, corn, a potato. "Fismon woman eat good," he said, shaking his head yes.

"These are lovely sketches," Mrs. Fitsimmons said. "Just look at these, Henry. Charming little pictures."

"They's good."

Shanti made a big fuss out of cooking the fish. He took out the fish livers and pointed to Mrs. Fitsimmons while he fixed them, boiling them slowly in a steel pot. He got her to understand that she should eat them every day. He sliced slivers of bark from the willow branches, covered them with water and boiled a tea for her to drink.

After we ate, he had Mrs. Fitsimmons lie on the bed while he pressed around on her. Mr. Fitsimmons wasn't real easy about it but he didn't say anything. We sat at the table, and I tried to draw some pictures on the paper. They looked like something a very stupid person would do.

"They'll try the horse thief first in the morning, Reece. Then you."

"Where do they do it?"

"Over at Lizzy's. They try and get through it quick as they can so they can go to drinking. No drinking till the judge is done."

"Do you think Kathryn will be there?"

"I 'spect everybody'll be there. Whole town and then some. Best you don't even look for Kathryn."

"Why not?"

"She's not the right kind for you, Reece, and it's no use wanting something you can't have. They's plenty women in this world."

"How long have you been married, Mr. Fitsimmons?"

"Twenty-three years."

Mrs. Fitsimmons said, "Twenty-four, Henry."

"When you first met her, did you know right away that you wanted to marry her?"

"No, that's fairy-tale stuff. Don't happen that way. I liked her right off and thought she was pretty, but it takes a while to know if you love somebody or not."

"How long does it take?"

"I don't know, something like six months, I guess. It happens kind of slow. Builds up, sorta sneaks up on you." He turned toward the bed. "How long it take you, Cora?"

"I'm still not so sure," she said. Then she laughed. "I didn't like him much at first, Herbert. He was so shy, for one thing. You say hello to him and he'd go to swallering and sliding his feet around."

It was hard to imagine Mr. Fitsimmons being shy.

"I know Kathryn's pulling at you, Reece," Mr. Fitsimmons said. "I know you're feeling sickly about her and ever thing, and I ain't being mean when I tell you that you'll get over it. Ever body kind of falls in love with their first girl. You just go ahead and feel stinking for a while, get it outa your insides, and then go on and find another girl. Find you a Cora."

Shanti and Mrs. Fitsimmons came over to the table and took chairs. Shanti looked at the pictures I had tried to draw. He said one of his new words: "Bad."

He began drawing over my pencil scribbles. He drew a lodge with a man and woman standing outside.

"House, Shanti, Mondala." He drew some little figures in a row beside the two larger people.

"He wants to get married and have lots of children," Mrs. Fitsimmons said.

I pointed to the small figures. "Children," I said. "Kids."

Shanti held up four fingers.

"Four children," I said.

He said, "Fole chillen."

~25~

I didn't sleep very well because I was scared. In the morning Shanti wouldn't let Mrs. Fitsimmons eat bacon and eggs with us. She sipped willow tea and ate two biscuits.

Mr. Fitsimmons took out his watch every few minutes. "Judge Stark likes to start on time," he said. He stood and hitched on his suspenders. "I'll come get you when it's time. Stay here with Cora."

A half hour later I heard him stomping up the stairs. He opened the door, "You ready?"

"I guess so."

"Judge Stark's in a bad mood. Took him ten minutes to get the horse thief outen the way."

"What happened?"

"Hang him in the morning."

Mrs. Fitsimmons said, "My goodness."

My knees shook when we followed Mr. Fitsimmons down the back steps and started toward the street. Mr. Fitsimmons stopped walking and looked at us. I said, "What is it?"

"I'm just wondering," he said. He scratched at his jaw whiskers. "Come on, let's get your horse saddled."

I said, "What for?" but he was already moving toward the stable. I waved for Shanti to follow, and we caught up with him at the door.

"I ain't going to let them hang you. If things go again you in there, I want you to be ready to make a run. You and Shanti."

I tossed on Packy's blanket and saddle. Shanti held Asham's head and spoke to him.

"We'll see how it goes, Reece. You be ready, just in case. If I give you a poke in the side, be ready to run for it."

"Okay."

"Maybe it'll go good for you, I don't know. If it don't, we want to have a way out."

I had never seen so many horses in Macland. The saloon was packed and noisy. We walked through the crowd toward the back. A desk had been brought from somewhere, and a slender middle-aged man sat behind it smoking a cigar. He had on a black robe that was shiny, like a crow's wing.

Chairs were in rows facing the desk. Mr. Fitsimmons pointed to seats along the right front row, and I sat down. Shanti sat beside me and said, "Chaya."

At the other end of the row of chairs were Little Sam, One-Eared Colby, and two soldiers. I turned and looked the crowd over. I guessed fifty people, most all men. A few saloon girls were there, but not Kathryn. I looked to my left and up to the top of the stairs and wondered if she was in her room. I wondered if she was alone. I wondered what was going to happen to me.

Sheriff Ames came through the doors and walked straight to the front. He nodded at me, handed Mr. Fitsimmons a dollar, and walked up to the desk. I heard him tell the judge, "Everybody's here."

The judge raised a wooden hammer and banged the desktop. "Everybody sit down and shut up." It got quiet real quick. A few chairs scraped the floor, someone coughed. "Bring in the jury, Ames."

A hand touched my shoulder. I turned and saw Dan. I nodded to him, and he smiled and sat next to Shanti. Sheriff Ames walked back in with six men following. They sat to my right in a row of chairs set sideways.

The judge dropped his cigar into a brass spittoon and whacked the desk again. "Court is in session. Judge Richard Stark presiding. That's me." He pointed with his hammer handle. "I want an orderly courtroom. No talking, no moving around. You have to leave for nature's calling, you do it quiet."

He went through some papers on his desk. Then he said, "The People versus Herbert R. Reece on the charge of murder." He looked up over his papers. "The defendant will stand."

Mr. Fitsimmons touched my arm, and I stood up. If we had to run, I wasn't sure that my legs would work.

Judge Stark said, "Mr. Reece, you are charged with the murder of Marshal Albert Combs on March eighteenth of this year. How do you plead?"

I said, "What do you mean?"

"How do you plead? Guilty or not guilty?"

"I'm not guilty."

The judge looked at the jury. "They always say that." He turned back to me and said, "Sit down. Sheriff, how come the defendant isn't shackled?"

Sheriff Ames stood. "I didn't think it was necessary, Your Honor."

"You didn't, uh? You know what the law says, don't you? The law specifies that murder suspects be shackled and restrained. As I understand, this man has already escaped twice."

"Yes, sir. But, he come back on his own and give hisself up, so I thought . . . The thing about it is, Judge. I don't think he done it anyhow, and I—"

"Shut up." The judge's face got red. "Come up here, Ames."

The sheriff walked up to the desk and leaned over to talk in whispers to the judge. The six men in the jury were talking back and forth to each other. The judge gave the desk another whack, easier this time. "All right, now, listen to me." He pointed his hammer handle at the jury. "The things the sheriff just said, I want you to forget it. He wasn't under oath, and what he said don't count." He gave the six men a hard look.

I glanced over at Shanti. He felt my eyes on him and turned to look back at me.

"Put your hand on the Bible."

Sheriff Ames put one hand on the Bible.

"Other hand, Ames."

The sheriff swapped hands.

"You swear to tell the truth, so help you God?"

"I do."

"Sit down."

The sheriff settled into an armchair by the side of the desk. Judge Stark said, "Now, you tell the jury what happened and just the facts. Don't be giving no opinions, just the facts."

"Well, couple weeks ago those two over there come into town with the body of Marshal Combs. Their names are Sam Aiken and Filmore Colby. They told me they had captured a Indian kid that was stealing horses from the fort and was bringing him in, taking him back to the fort and this here boy"—he pointed to me—"they said he surprised them. They said he shot Combs in the back and took their guns and horses and rode off with the Indian."

The judge said, "Did you examine the body?"

"Yes, sir."

"What did he die of?"

"Let's see, I guess he died of a Wednesday."

"No, what was the cause of his death?"

"He'd been back-shot, twice."

The judge said, "What transpired next?"

"He was already transpired, Judge. Already cold and stiff."

"What happened next, Sheriff?"

"Well, we went looking for Reece, the four of us, and saw him riding out. We formed up a posse and followed him quick as we could, and there was a hell of a blizzard. Couldn't hardly see nothing, but his tracks was fresh. About three miles out a town, why *boom*, *boom*, there's these two shots and we pull up. Ole Eugene Ledbetter, he didn't stop in time and crashed into a big ole cedar that had blown down and cracked this here bone slap in two." Ames rubbed across his collarbone.

He turned around to look at the judge. "The kid here had tried to warn us, shooting that away. He hadn't shot we'd a all piled into that tree. Somebody coulda been kilt."

The judge nodded. "Go on, Sheriff, and just tell what happened."

"Well, we had to take Eugene back, get him took care of, and the blizzard was fiercer. Next day we took out after him again, and Dan here, he tracked him two days and we found him and he give himself up peaceful and said he didn't kill nobody. He said those two probably done Combs in." He pointed to Colby and Little Sam. "Reece said what really happened was that—"

The judge tapped his hammer. "We'll hear from the defendant later, Sheriff. You just tell what happened next."

"You don't want me to tell about the things was said around the fire?"

"No, that's irrelevant."

"We all figured them two was lying." He pointed to Little Sam and Colby.

"Just what happened, Sheriff, not what you thought."

Ames spoke softly, almost to himself. "Lying like hell, you ask me."

The judge laid into the desk with that hammer and made me jump in the chair. Shanti laughed about it. The judge's face was red again. "Dammit, Ames, you know how to give testimony. You stay with the facts, or I'm going to hold you in contempt and put you in your own damned jail."

The sheriff said, "Well, Dan thought they was lying too. He got up close in their face and looked at their eyes and—"

The judge crashed his hammer down again. "All right, that's enough." He stood up. "The court is taking a recess. You all take care of nature if you need to. Be back here in ten minutes. Sheriff, you come with me."

The sheriff looked at the jury men. "Dan can always tell. Some kind of Indian thing."

❧ 26 ❧

Shanti and I walked around to the back of Lizzy's saloon and used the outhouse. Colby stepped up between us on our way back. "You tell us where the gold is, boy, or you'll hang tomorrow."

I kept walking. "Last chance," he said.

Shanti reached up to touch Colby's head where his ear was gone. Colby slapped his hand away.

I said, "Who shot Combs, you or Sam?"

"It don't matter, does it?"

We stepped onto the boardwalk. Shanti was looking at the side of Colby's head. Colby put his hand over his missing ear and said, "Stop it."

I said, "I figure it was you, since it was in the back."

Colby turned around so that his right side was toward Shanti. That was the side that had an ear on it. He said, "If they don't hang you, I'll kill you myself. Maybe in your sleep. Maybe when you're riding along by yourself somewhere. Maybe when—"

I said, "Can you hear out of that little hole?"

He covered his ear and stomped away quickly, all red in the face. I knew it wasn't nice to make fun of somebody's missing parts, but I liked doing it anyway. We went into Lizzy's and took our seats. Four of the jury men were sitting. I looked them over, and one of them, a young fellow of twenty or so, gave me a wink.

Sheriff Ames sat back in his chair. The judge stood behind his desk and whacked it three times. When everyone had settled down, he walked over in front of the jury men and gave them each a long look. "Now, listen to me, people. We got us a murder trial here, and here's what we know so far. We know a federal marshal's been shot. We know these two deputy marshals brought in the body and said the defendant over there did the dirty deed."

He pointed at me, then turned back to the six men. "We also know that the defendant ran away. I want you to forget the rest of it, what the sheriff thought. We're not interested in what the sheriff thought, just what he saw and heard. You understand that?" He looked them over, and they nodded their heads.

"There has been a murder done, a murder of a federal marshal, and we owe it to him to see somebody hangs for it." He walked back behind his desk and sat down. "All right, Sheriff, you're still under oath. Now, you lit out for Reece after the storm passed through and caught up with him. Is that right?"

"Yes, sir."

"And then he escaped again?"

"Yes, sir. Well, not exactly, not what you'd call escape exactly, it was more like he got rescued."

"The Indians helped him escape, is that it?"

"Well, yeah. But, see, what happened, the kid here, Reece, he talked them into letting us go. You might say he sorta rescued us. I think the Indians were of a mind to do us in."

"I don't want you to tell us what you think, Sheriff. I

thought I explained that to you. The defendant escaped again, correct?"

"Naw, he just sorta rode off with his friends, Judge."

"Did you tell him he was no longer under arrest?"

"No, can't say as I did."

"Then he escaped."

Sheriff Ames turned toward the jury and whispered, "Just rode off."

"That's enough." The judge looked at me. "Do you have any questions to ask this witness?"

I said, "About what?"

"You have the right to ask him questions. It's called cross-examination. You don't have to ask him anything, but you can if you want to."

I thought a moment. "Yeah, there is one thing I'd like to ask him."

"Proceed."

"Do you know what happened to Colby's ear?"

Sheriff Ames said, "Way I heard it, he was—"

The judge banged his hammer down. "The question is improper and irrelevant to these proceedings. Step down, Ames." The judge looked at his papers. "Next witness is Sam Aiken."

Little Sam put his hand on the Bible and said, "I do."

The judge asked him to tell what happened on March eighteenth, and Little Sam said, "Well, some Injuns raided the corral and stole a pack of horses. It was early, just breaking daylight, and me and Combs and Colby took out after them."

Little Sam kept his head down as he spoke. "We come up on them just other side of Simm's Creek. There was four of 'em and this one here," he raised his head and pointed at Shanti, "he was trailing the others half a mile and saw us coming and took off to warn the others, and we all shot at him. Somebody, one of us, hit his horse, and it went down, and we chased him down."

Dan was whispering to Shanti as Sam spoke. Shanti was shaking his head back and forth.

Little Sam said, "The others, they heard the shots, and we know'd we'd never catch up to them, so we started back to the fort with our prisoner. Injun scouts at the fort, we figured they could talk to the kid and tell him how it was wrong to steal horses and if they brought them back, there's no hard feelings."

Judge Stark said, "You meant the man no harm, is that correct?"

"That's right, Judge. We just wanted to explain him the error of his ways."

Dan whispered to Shanti, and Shanti laughed out loud. He had the kind of laugh that made me have to laugh along with him. The judge slammed his hammer down and gave us a mean look. I quit laughing, but Shanti was having trouble with it and had to press his hands over his mouth. The young guy in the jury was smiling, and he winked at me again.

"Go on, Deputy Aiken. What happened next?"

"Well, we stopped under some trees by a creek to rest our horses. Seeing as we was one horse short and had to ride double, we figured we'd rest the horses awhile and give the prisoner something to eat. Up rides the kid here and we asked him, we told him, we'd give him something to eat. We didn't have much food, but we figured we'd just go hungry ourselves. Get the young fellows fed."

Dan whispered to Shanti, and Shanti went to laughing again. The judge banged his hammer, and Shanti tried to stop but didn't make it, and slid down in his chair with his hands over his face. It got me started laughing, too, and soon we were giggling and squealing like girls in church.

Wham, again. "I'll have the sheriff gag you both, you don't keep still there. This here's a murder trial, dammit."

It hurt. I quit laughing, but it hurt. I didn't dare look at Shanti or I would have broken loose again. When I looked away, I saw Kathryn sitting at the top of the stairs dressed real pretty. She looked back at me for a few seconds, then dropped her eyes.

Little Sam was talking again, ". . . turned around and Combs was lying facedown and the kid was holding a pistol. Made us throw our guns down, and after he went through our gear, he rode off with the Injun and our horses."

The judge said, "It was cold-blooded murder, then."

"That's right."

The judge looked at me. "You have any questions?"

Before I could answer, Mr. Fitsimmons said, "I'd like to ask him something, Judge."

"Who are you?"

"Henry Fitsimmons. I own the trading post here in Macland."

The judge said, "It okay with you, Mr. Reece?"

"Yes, sir."

"Go ahead, then."

Mr. Fitsimmons walked over to Little Sam and stood in front of him with his arms crossed on his chest. "You're a lying son of a bitch, Sam."

Wham. "That's enough of that. You can ask him questions and that's all. No name-calling."

Mr. Fitsimmons said, "When did you whip the Indian boy?"

Little Sam said, "I didn't whip nobody. I don't know nothing about no whipping. I don't know nothing about them scars on him."

"How'd you know there's scars?"

"Well," Little Sam shifted around in the chair and looked toward Colby, then the judge, then at the floor. "I mean, if there's some scars on him, I don't know nothing about them."

"You don't even know if there are any scars, is that right?"

"That's right."

"Well, Little Sam, you done gone and shit in your own hat. The boy showed us all his scars when he and the other warriors caught up with us at the pass. You saw them then. I saw them, so did the sheriff and Dan and Biggs."

"Well, I don't know where they come from's what I mean."

The judge said, "It doesn't matter anyhow. This here isn't a whipping trial. It's a murder trial. Deputy Aikens isn't accused of anything."

"Yeah, but he's doing some accusing, ain't he? I figure a man lies about whipping, he lies about other things too. I don't believe a damn word he said so far."

"Well, you aren't on the jury."

"If I was, I'd figure this'n for a skunk and a liar."

Wham. "Shut up and sit down. No more questions."

Mr. Fitsimmons grumbled to himself as he sat back down next to me. I said, "That was real good." Kathryn was looking down at me, just looking.

"Next witness is Deputy Filmore Colby."

·27·

Colby told his story about the same as Little Sam, except he left out the part about giving us the last of their food because they were so kind-hearted. I was hoping he would tell it again so Shanti would laugh and slide down in his chair some more. I spent a lot of time looking up at Kathryn, but she didn't look back.

"Do you have any questions for this man?"

"Yeah," Mr. Fitsimmons said. "I got some."

When I looked up the stairs, Kathryn was gone.

Mr. Fitsimmons said, "You didn't whip the Indian, did you, Colby?"

"No."

"You ever whip anybody?"

"Done some fighting," Colby said. "Whipped some guys with my fists. Been whipped myself a few times."

"You ever beat up a woman?"

The judge said, "Now you're starting up on that whipping business again. Told you before, this ain't a whipping trial, ain't a woman-beating trial. It's a murder trial, because that boy Reece shot Marshal Combs in the back."

"You ain't supposed to say that, Judge. You ain't supposed to say someone's guilty or nothing."

"Whose court is this, Fitsimmons? Yours or mine?"

"It's your court, but—"

"You got a question about the murder, ask it. Otherwise shut up. These men ain't had a drink all day."

There was some talk from the crowd behind me. Fitsimmons turned toward the jury men. "I got a barrel of applejack in the store that's better than anything. You say the boy's not guilty and we'll all get cross-eyed and won't cost you nothing."

Wham. "Fitsimmons, that was a bribe of the jury. Now, dammit, I can't allow that. You know I can't allow that."

"But this here's a fine young fellow, Judge. I knowed his father and—"

Wham. "The court fines you one barrel of applejack."

"Aw, shit, Judge."

"And sit down. You're not helping Reece any, and you're making me mad. I'll have Ames carry you to jail, you rankle me one more time."

Mr. Fitsimmons grumbled to himself and sat next to me.

The judge said, "Any more questions for this witness here? You got anything to ask, Reece?"

I started to say no, but Mr. Fitsimmons tugged my shirt sleeve and leaned close. "Ask him some more. Keep him up there talking and see if you can get him to slip up."

"What should I ask him?"

"Anything. Get him sore if you can. More the jury sees of him, the better. Just keep him talking."

I said, "He'll just keep lying, Mr. Fitsimmons."

"Lying's hard to do, longer you do it, the harder to keep track of everything."

"Okay." I stood up and walked over to Colby and looked at his ear hole. "How much gold did Shanti have with him when he saw the general?"

"I don't know anything about no gold."

I said, "Weren't you there when he met with the general?"

"No, he didn't see the general. He and the others, they just come to steal horses."

"How much gold did he have?"

"I told you. I don't know nothing about no gold. I don't know anything about a map neither."

"What map?" I leaned forward to get a better look down his hole. "I didn't say anything about a map."

"You was about to."

"No, I wasn't."

"Yeah, you were."

"What map did you mean?"

"The map that showed . . . There ain't no map."

"Yes, there is. I've seen the map, Colby."

"Well, it won't do you no good."

"Why not?"

"Because it's . . . I mean, there ain't no map, and that's what I'm saying."

"Well, I saw a map. What do you figure it was?"

"Just some scratching, some lines on paper."

"What paper?"

"There ain't no paper either."

I said, "After you shot Marshal Combs, did you go through his saddlebags?"

"You the one shot Combs," Colby said. He leaned back and smiled at me, then over at Little Sam.

"Well, after he was dead, did you go through his saddlebags?"

"No."

"Did Sam?"

"No."

"What did you do, just throw the saddlebags away?"

"No, but . . . What I mean is, if we looked in his bags, we didn't find nothing. No gold or nothing."

"They were empty, huh?"

"Yeah. I don't know. Maybe some cartridges or something."

"Who looked, you or Sam?"

"I don't know. Yeah, it was Sam."

"What did he find?"

"Nothing."

"Maybe he found something and didn't tell you."

"Like what?"

"Something like a map, some gold."

"No, he didn't find nothing."

I was running out of things to ask, and my throat was dry from all the talking. I walked over to the table where Little Sam and the two soldiers were sitting and poured a glass of water from their pitcher.

The judge said, "Are you done asking questions, Mr. Reece?"

"No, not yet." I set down the glass and wiped my hands on my trousers. I felt the gold in my right-hand pocket and got an idea. Sam was watching me close. I leaned down toward him and, while he was watching my face, took a chunk out of my pocket, keeping it closed up in a fist. "Think I'm going to hang, Sam?"

"Yep, and I'm gonna watch."

My back was to Colby and the judge. I said, "Well, no hard feelings," and stuck out my hand. Little Sam tried to shake hands, but I kept my fist shut. I turned around and opened my hand as if Little Sam had handed me something.

I said, "What's this?" and did some play-acting. I frowned real big as I walked over to Colby, looking down at the gold rock in my palm. When Colby saw it, his eyes got big and his face turned red.

"Sam, you son of a bitch. What are you . . . ?" He turned to the judge. "It was him that done it." He pointed at Little Sam.

The judge said, "Done what?"

Sam stood up, knocking his chair backward. "Shut up, Colby. Just shut up."

Colby stood too. "You can't cross me, Sam. Not now you can't. Not never."

The judge was banging his hammer, and everybody was talking at once, even the jury men. I glanced up and saw Kathryn. She smiled and turned to walk away down the hallway. She was just about perfect.

It took a lot of desk banging to get everybody quiet and sat back down. Shanti was having a good time, and so was Mr. Fitsimmons. He slapped my back. "You done good, Reece."

The judge said, "This court is adjourned for lunch. All meet back here in one hour." He whacked the desk again.

◆ 28 ◆

When we got back in the courtroom the judge had me sit in the witness chair, and I told him and the jury how it really happened. Nobody asked me any questions, and I sat back down.

Shanti was next. The judge told Dan, "Ask him if he knows what the Bible is."

After some Yahi talk, Dan said, "He calls it 'The New Book of Heaven.' "

"Well, ask him if he believes in it."

After more talk Dan said, "Shanti say he believes about the Big Chief in Sky. No believe Jonah man live in big fish."

"Close enough." The judge turned to the jury. "Just remember, these people lie, they're brought up that way."

Shanti went over the whole story with Dan's help. I watched the jury men's faces, and I think they believed him. The judge told Shanti to sit back down, then gathered up his robes and walked over in front of the six jury men. "Now, it shouldn't take long for you people to make up your mind." He walked up and down in front of the men, looking at their faces as he talked. "Here's what we got. We got two deputies here says that Reece done the killing. They got no reason to lie. Now, Reece here tries to make it out that they done the shooting. Why would they do that? And another thing. If they had done the shooting, why didn't they just bury the marshal and nobody'd know no better? They didn't do that. What they did was the proper thing, and legal. They brought in the body, real respectful like, and made their charges to the sheriff."

Mr. Fitsimmons whispered to me. "Looks bad, Reece."

The judge said, "Now, on the other side you got Reece telling some story about gold and maps and what all. Try and confuse you. Remember, a guilty man always says somebody else done it, so you can't much believe him." He turned and pointed to Shanti. "And we all know that heathens lie, so what he said don't count for much."

He backed off and stared the jury down for half a minute. "Now, you all go back there and vote on it. Don't be taking a real long time about it. You know what your duty is and—"

"Wait a minute." We all looked up. Kathryn was coming down the steps. "Just wait a minute, Judge. I want to sit in that chair and say something."

"And who might you be, Miss?"

"Kathryn Rose Forrest." She walked through the crowd and picked up the Bible.

"You a whore?"

"I sure am. A good one, too, which is more than I can say about you and your judging."

The judge drew his mouth down. "I sure don't need a whore to tell me about judging."

"Well, you need somebody to tell you." She laid the

Bible on the desk and raised her little hand, "I, Kathryn Rose Forrest swear to tell the truth, the whole truth, and nothing but the truth, so help me God." She plopped down in the chair, looked at the judge, and said, "Well, sit down."

The judge walked around behind his desk. "Do you know something about this case?"

"Yes, I do."

"Well, I don't know how the jury will believe you, being a whore, but go ahead and say your piece."

Kathryn turned toward the six men. "There's been some lying going on from this chair. Colby and Aikens both been lying to you. Especially Aikens. The only time Aikens isn't lying to you is when his mouth is shut."

"You let the jury decide who is lying for themselves, young lady. You just tell what you know, then go sit down. Or lay down." The judge smiled at his remark and some of the men laughed from the saloon.

Kathryn went right on like she hadn't heard. "There's two times a man tells the truth, when he's dumb drunk is one time. Other time is when he's with a woman alone and she tells him how wonderful he is, sweet-talks him about how he is better than all the other men and everything. A man hears that and he'll always believe it, tell you the truth."

The judge said, "Say what you have to say, Miss."

"All right, I'm getting to it now. Aikens has been hanging around Lizzy's, drinking and gambling and shooting his mouth off about how he's going to get the kid here hung. One night he's so drunk and he decides he wants to buy some of my time, so we go upstairs with a bottle and get in bed and all that. He's pretty drunk, and after while he passes out.

"When he wakes up, I tell him, 'Oh, Sam, you're so

wonderful. I never knew a man like you before.' I say, 'It was so wonderful I don't want your money.'

"Sam says he wants me to be his woman and nobody else's. He says he will have plenty of money soon, and I tell him I wished I could believe him 'cause he is such a real man, and that's when he told me about the gold. Told me about the Indians coming to the fort with gold and a map, just like Shanti told it. He told me about the Reece kid saving the Indian boy when they was about to hang him. Just like Reece told it himself.

"I give him another drink and let him feel my titty and he tells me how Colby shot the marshal and how they plan to get the kid blamed for it so's they can get him to tell where the gold is."

"That's all lies," Little Sam shouted from his chair.

"It's true, what I told you," Kathryn said to the jury men. She looked real pretty sitting up there.

Colby stood up and walked toward Kathryn. "You're just lying 'cause you're sweet on Reece. You're just trying to get back at me 'cause I roughed you up some. Ain't that right?"

Kathryn shook her head.

"You no good slut, I shoulda killed you. I shoulda messed up your face so's no man would ever look at you no more. I'm gonna do it one day, you remember that."

I got up, and Colby turned to me, crouched down, and pulled a long skinning knife from inside his boot. "Come on, kid." He wiggled his fingers at me. "Come on."

The judge banged his hammer, and Sheriff Ames drew his gun, pointed it at Colby, and said, "Drop it."

Shanti was standing next to me, and Indian Dan was circling to get behind Colby. The judge said, "Nobody move." When I glanced at him, he had a shotgun pointed our way. He clicked back both hammers. "You folks all sit down."

I itched for a chance to get at Colby, but sat down. The judge laid the shotgun across the desk. He said, "Now, what the little whore said don't count. Aikens had his say under oath, that's what counts. What this girl said was secondhand, called hearsay, and it don't mean anything."

Kathryn said, "It's called the rule of best evidence."

Judge Stark frowned. "How'd you know that?"

"My daddy's a judge. A real judge, in Saint Louis."

"Then you know that your testimony was improper."

Kathryn nodded. "Yes, but Daddy, he always said that juries mostly end up doing the right thing if they get the chance."

"They'll get their chance. Now, you get off that chair."

I watched her walk across the room and climb the stairs full of sass. She sat down on the top step. I whispered, "She did that for me, Mr. Fitsimmons. I'll bet that's why she played up to Little Sam."

The judge whipsawed the jury some more about how they had to find me guilty, and sent them out of the room. Indian Dan and Shanti were talking a lot back and forth. So were Colby and Aikens. So were Mr. Fitsimmons and Sheriff Ames. The judge got another cigar going and put his feet up on the desk.

I walked up to him, and he smiled at me. I didn't expect that. I said, "Could I ask you something about law?"

"Sure, what you need, Reece?"

"Is it true that Indians can't own land?"

"Yep. I can't quote you the statute off the top of my head, but that's true."

"Doesn't seem right."

"Isn't right. It's the law, though. They really do know where there's gold, huh?"

"Yes. I told the truth up there."

He quick-puffed his cigar and admired the ash. "Just doing my job, you know. I got nothing against you."

"What do you do, get paid by the hanging or something?"

"No, straight salary. What you could do, Reece, you could buy land and lease it to your Indian friends."

"Lease it?"

"Sure, that's what I'd do. Buy the land, you being a white man, then rent it to them for a dollar a year, and everything is nice and legal. Just fill out some papers is all."

"Would you show me how?"

"Yeah, if I don't hang you tomorrow, I'll help you set it all up." He glanced up the steps. "Tonight I plan to drink a while and thump on that little whore up there."

"Well, I . . . ah—"

"Here they come, Reece. Sit down and let's see what they got to say."

The young man on the jury gave me a wink on the way to his chair. A man the judge called the foreman said, "We find the defendant not guilty."

The judge banged his desk. "Defendant is free to go." He banged it again. "Bartender, I'll have a whiskey."

◆ 29 ◆

There were some men I had never seen before who felt obliged to shake my hand and thump me on the back. A lot of hard drinking and loud talking had broken out. I finally worked my way to the steps and took them two at a time. I knocked on Kathryn's door, shuffled my feet, knocked some more, and coughed a few times. There was silence from the room, but it didn't sound empty.

I knocked again. "Kathryn?" I got my face closer to the door. "Thanks for what you did down there, Kathryn. Thanks for sitting in that chair and what you said. It sure did help."

More silence. "Come on, Kathryn, say something."

The silence got louder. "Are you mad at me?" And louder. "What did I do? . . . Was it something I said? . . . Are you sick?"

None of that worked. I said, "Kathryn, I feel really dumb standing here and talking to a door."

Her voice came softly. "Please go away."

"Can't I see you?"

"No, go away."

"Are you mad at me or something?"

"No. I just don't want to see you for a while, or anybody."

"Could I see you later maybe?"

"No. Go away, Reece."

"But I . . . thanks for what you said."

"Just go away."

"I . . ."

"Please."

"Are you all right?"

"Yes, leave me alone."

I scuffed down the hall and stood at the top of the steps, looking back. The door seemed to grow bigger while I watched it. Bigger and thicker and more shut. I went down the steps and out of the saloon. Men were at work on the street building a gallows.

Shanti had Mrs. Fitsimmons on the bed again, touching around on her joints. "There's food on the stove, Herbert," she said.

I fixed a plate and picked around on it. Mrs. Fitsimmons was teaching Shanti more words. They laughed together. I knew it was a happy sound, but I couldn't take the feeling inside.

Dad had said that a man was better not to eat when he was real mad or real sad. "Food just angers up the blood when you force it down through sour feelings," he had said. I walked to the stove and scraped the food back into the pots.

"Aren't you hungry, Herbert?"

"No, I guess not. It was good, though. I'm just not hungry."

"The excitement," she said. "All that happened. You can eat later."

"Yes, ma'am. I think I'll see the horses."

Shanti said, "Leece see Packy, Leece see Asham."

"That's right, Shanti."

Mrs. Fitsimmons said, "Shanti is a very intelligent young man, Herbert."

"I know."

Packy was glad to see me, and so was Asham. I gave them both a good brushdown while I told them about Kathryn.

"Best thing, when you're all down and sad about something is to go ahead and allow yourself to be that way," Dad had told me. "Just go ahead and waller in it, like a pig in the mud. Then get up and go about making things better again."

I wallered around in it for a while, then walked up to the front of Fitsimmons's store. He had some customers, and I busied myself with a broom, sweeping from the back toward the front. It hadn't been done in a long time.

When I got done sweeping, I found some paper and pencil and wrote my mom and sister a long letter. When the customers left, Mr. Fitsimmons sat down next to me. "Here's your check for the furs."

"Thank you."

"How's Kathryn?"

I shrugged. "Didn't want to see me. Wouldn't open the door."

"Oh."

"Kept saying, 'Go away.' "

"Bet that felt stinkin'."

"Uh-huh."

"What's your plans, Reece?"

"I don't know. Talk to the judge tomorrow."

"About what?"

"Shanti, Shanti and his people and the gold and how

to get them some land of their own. He says there's a way."

Some more men came in the store. I finished the letter, stuck in the check, and sealed it up. The man at the post office wanted to talk about where the gold was, and I told him I didn't know anything about it. Sometimes the easiest thing to do is just go ahead and lie.

I looked in at Lizzy's. The judge was at the bar with a red face and a girl at his side. Kathryn wasn't there. I walked back to the stables and talked with Packy some more until it got dark.

Shanti and Mrs. Fitsimmons were still at it. He was rubbing her knees after he dipped his hands in the willow tea. I ate a little bit of stew and listened to them talk.

Mr. Fitsimmons came up and sat with me, eating stew with a great big spoon. He made a lot of slurp noise, and Mrs. Fitsimmons said, "I should get you a trough, Henry." After that he quieted down his eating some.

"How you feeling, Reece?"

"All right."

"Want to play some cards, take your mind off it?"

"Yeah."

"Come on."

We walked to Lizzy's and got a table in the back. Biggs sat down with us along with Dan, Sheriff Ames, and Lizzy herself. Lizzy was well fed. She wore a fancy dress cut low at the top to show all the bosom she could. It looked like a baby's behind. We played a few hands before she said, "Pay attention to your cards, young man. Quit watching the stairs. She's not coming down."

"Why not?"

Lizzy opened for a dime. "I don't know. Been locked in her room all day. Says she's leaving."

Everyone called. I held a pair of sevens and drew three cards. "Leaving for where?"

"Back where she came from. Saint Louis."

"When?"

Lizzy said, "Bet a dime. When's the stage, Sheriff?"

"Four, five days. What do you do, Reece?"

I had two pair, sevens and fours. "Call."

Sheriff Ames called.

"Three queens," Lizzy said. She raked in the pot. "That's life, Reece. You win some, you lose some."

We played a few more hands. Dan and Lizzy did most of the winning. The judge came down the steps with one of the girls. He looked pleased with himself. He headed for our table and sat next to Lizzy. "Fine place you got here, ma'am. Whose deal?"

"It's yours, Tomcat." Lizzy grinned.

Judge Stark shuffled the cards. "Now, that feisty little lady you got working here, you're going to have to teach her be nicer, good customers like me."

Lizzy said, "She treat you bad, Sugar?"

"Sure did." He looked at me. "Pulled your neck out of a rope and made me look bad front of everybody. Now she won't let me in her bed. I was you, Lizzy, I'd talk to her."

Lizzy said, "I don't own these girls, Lover Boy. You don't really want someone who don't want you, do you?"

He began dealing, " 'Course I do, I'm willing to pay."

After a few more hands Lizzy dropped out. We played for an hour. The judge and Biggs were poor players and never folded, staying for most every showdown. Dan, Mr. Fitsimmons, and I gradually won their money, and Biggs went bust and quit. I was feeling bad about taking from the judge and wanted to quit, too, but he fussed about it and demanded a chance to get his money back.

He lost some more and drank some more. Mr. Fitsimmons told some good jokes, but the judge didn't laugh. He wanted to raise the ante and limit, and after we agreed to it, he lost faster.

I said, "Deal me out."

"You ain't quitting with all my money," the judge said.

Mr. Fitsimmons said, "Let him go." He shuffled the cards. "One time this old man come riding into town on a mule. . . ."

Lizzy was standing with her back to the bar, leaning on her elbows. I went over to her. "Have you got a key to Kathryn's room?"

She shook her head. "Locks from the inside."

"How much are those doors?"

"What do you mean, how much?"

"I mean, if I break it down, how much would it cost?"

"Oh, hell, Reece. Don't go breaking down any doors." She gave me a sad like smile. You could tell that Lizzy had been real pretty when she was young. There was still some of the pretty left too. "Why don't you and I go upstairs and have a little party, just you and me?"

"Well, I really would sort of like to talk to Kathryn."

"I'd make you forget all about that little split-tail."

"Thanks and all that, but if I could just talk to her . . ."

"You afraid of me?"

"No."

"You think you're in love with Kathryn, don't you?"

"I don't know. Yeah, I mean I like her and think about her all the time."

She shook her head. "Your first girl, everybody thinks they're in love with their first girl. It'll ease off. I could ease it off you in about twenty minutes, half hour." She reached out her hand and squeezed my privates, which was something I never would have expected.

"Don't do that, Miss Lizzy." I backed away and looked around. Nobody had seen it.

"Your face is all red, Reece."

"You surprised me is all."

"I got lots of surprises for you. You'd think you'd died and gone to heaven. You wouldn't have to do anything, just lie there."

"Come on, Miss Lizzy. Don't talk that way."

She turned and finished off her whiskey drink. I said, "What do you mean, just lie there?"

"Just what I said. I'd do all the work."

"But how do you . . . ? I mean, what . . . ?"

"I'll show you. Trust me."

"Would you see if you could get Kathryn to see me?"

"Okay, Reece, tell you what. You put your arm around me, and we'll walk up the stairs. I'll see if I can get her to open that door. If she don't, my room's right down the hall."

We started toward the stairs. I put my arm on her, and she leaned against me with her head on my shoulder. It was kind of nice. There was some hooting from the men at the bar. One guy said, "Robbing the cradle, ain't you, Lizzy?" Everybody thought that was pretty funny. Lizzy put her arm around my waist as we climbed the steps. "How come you're always looking down my dress, Reece?"

"What?"

"You like what you see down there, is that it?"

"No, ma'am."

"You don't?"

"Well, I mean. Sure, you're nice to look at." We reached the top of the stairs, and Lizzy turned and faced me. I looked over her head, down the hall at Kathryn's door.

Lizzy took my hand and pressed it against her breast. "Let's go to my room."

"Aw, Lizzy, let me talk to Kathryn, please." My hand was squeezing her breast. I didn't mean for it to, it just did it on its own. I jerked it away and put both hands in my pockets.

Lizzy shook her head and turned. I followed her down the hall. She rocked her hips back and forth for me, and I couldn't help but look. I wondered what she meant, "Just lie there." She knocked on Kathryn's door. "Open up, honey."

"What do you want?"

"We got us a sick puppy out here needs to see you."

The latch clicked, the door opened, and there she was. I looked at her, and she looked at me. Lizzy slapped my backside. "Give it a try, kid."

⭒30⭒

Lizzy centered her hand between my shoulders and pushed. Kathryn had to step out of my way. Lizzy said, "She don't treat you right, you come see me, Reece." She shut the door, and Kathryn and I looked at each other.

There was a suitcase on the bed, half filled with frilly women things. I said, "Are you really going away?"

"Yes, I really am. I've made up my mind, Reece."

"Why?"

"Lots of reasons." She folded her arms. "A big reason is you, Reece."

"What do you mean, me?"

"Sit down, Reece, now that you're here. Sit on the sofa there."

Kathryn sat on the side of the bed. She looked at her lap for a moment. "You know, when I came out here, I thought, I told myself that with so few women around and all these men, well, I figured to meet me a man, a nice young man who would like me and maybe want to get married and have kids and everything. A house and all that."

She looked up. "Then you come along, and I knew that it wouldn't work."

"What do you mean?"

"Well, there you are. You're a nice young man. And you like me, I can tell it, and it's real nice, but it's just awful."

"What do you mean, awful?"

She shook her head. "It's just terrible. I was dumb to run away, coming out here, working for Lizzy, thinking I'd meet a fellow that way and make something of myself, of my life."

"I still don't understand. . . ."

"I've thought about it, Reece. Suppose, just suppose that we spent some time together and, you know, maybe really got to like each other and all and maybe even got married."

"Well . . ."

"No matter how good it was for us, you'd always know you'd married a whore."

"No, I wouldn't, Kathryn."

"Yes, you would. It would always be there in your head. I mean, everything would be fine, but you'd always think it, and I'd always know you thought it."

"No, Kathryn. It wouldn't—"

"Shush! It would be like that. Even if we were loving real nice, you would think about the others I've been with. Like that Sam Aikens. My God, Reece. I slept with Sam Aikens, you'd never get that out your head. And others just as bad. You would think and wonder about them."

"No, I wouldn't."

"Dammit, Reece, you sure would. Quit denying everything I say. You deny everything before you even think about it."

"No, I don't."

She looked at me. "You just did it again."

"No, I didn't."

She laughed. She had a nice laugh, and it made me smile, just hearing it. "Well, what I mean is—"

"Don't talk, Reece. Just think about what all I've just said and you'll see I'm right. It wouldn't be good. You ought to have it good. So should I. We'd end up miserable with each other."

"Kathryn, I . . ."

"Hush now. Hush up and ponder it."

I didn't say anything for a while, but I tried not to think about what she said. I was afraid she was right. Sam Aikens. The thought of her with him made me hurt behind my eyes. I guess there had been others, lots of others.

I said, "I still wish you'd stay."

"No."

"What if I asked . . . ?

"No!"

I looked at my hands awhile. "You really going back to Saint Louis?"

She nodded.

I nodded back. "When you leaving?"

"Saturday, whenever the stage comes through."

"Back with your dad?"

"He's all I have. How about you, Reece?"

"I don't know."

"I wish it was different, Reece. I wish it was different for us, you and me."

I nodded. "Me too. You think it'll be okay, living with your dad this time?"

"I'll make it work. I'm going to tell him about what you said."

"What was that?"

"That you can be whatever you want to be. You were right there, Reece. I'm going to tell Dad that I want to be a good woman and ask him to help me and not be telling me I'm no good and like my mother all the time."

"You're sure that's what you want to do?"

"I'm sure."

"This is sad."

"I know. You want to go now it's okay."

"I got nowhere to go. Can I help you pack or something?"

"No, I'm almost done."

I looked at her. "I do like you, Kathryn."

"I know. I know you feel bad, but it won't last forever. You better leave."

"I don't want to."

"The longer you stay, the worse it'll be. For my sake, you go on now."

I said, "Maybe we could write each other, you know, letters."

"That would be nice."

She got paper from her dresser and wrote down her address. I told her to write me in care of Mr. Fitsimmons. She let me hold her for a long time, and she held me back. She was so small and nice and fit right up against me. When we kissed, she fooled with the hair in back of my neck.

"Good-bye, Reece."

"You sure?"

"Yes."

It was cold in the hallway. I walked down the steps and saw Mr. Fitsimmons, Indian Dan, Sheriff Ames, and the judge, still playing cards. They didn't look like real people.

I walked by them. They looked up but didn't say anything. I checked on Packy and Asham before I climbed the steps. Shanti and Mrs. Fitsimmons were asleep, and I scooted into my cover without waking anybody.

❖31❖

"Take these here maps with you," the judge said. "And a compass. Use landmarks, like a tree or creek or something. If there aren't any, build yourself a monument marker. Pile up some rocks." He sipped coffee and looked around. People were finishing their breakfast and leaving the restaurant called Eat.

"Where do I start?"

"Anywhere. Like if it was here on this map. You make your mark and then draw a line up this way and write in something like, 'Starting from point A at rock pile, a line northeast to the oak tree, then west-southwest to the creek bed, then south to a large oak tree, then east to point A.'"

He went over it all again several times. I said, "So then I take it to the Land Office."

"Yep. If there's no previous claim, you can buy it and they'll fix you up a deed. Two deeds. They keep one, give you one. Then you write up a lease agreement like this one here I made out for you. Rent it to those Yahis for a dollar a year and you're all set."

"Thanks, judge." I rolled up all the papers.

"You staying for the hanging, ain't you?"

"No." I stood up and shook his hand. "Have you seen Little Sam or Colby around?"

"Saw them leave right after the trial, in a big hurry. Them and the soldiers. You better watch your back with them two, son."

"I will."

Shanti and I made our good-byes to the Fitsimmonses and rode through the crowd that was building around the gallows. Some people had their children with them. All the girls from Lizzy's were standing in front of the saloon. All except Kathryn, and I was glad she wasn't there. I wondered if she would write.

Shanti said, "Leece, Shanti go . . . ?"

"We ride to my cabin. My house. Reece *wowi*. Sleep. Ride to Shanti's *wowi*. Make marks on map."

"*Walama* map."

"That's right. Then we go and get lots of gold, the rocks of yellow, *el oro amarillo*. We give the gold rocks and get a paper that says the land is yours. *Walama* is Shanti's."

He looked at my face and nodded. We rode into the foothills. Shanti said, "Fismon man good. Fismon woman good."

"Yes, they are."

"No-ear man bad. Sam bad."

"You're right."

"Yahi man good. Yahi man bad."

"Yeah, I guess so. Have to take them one at a time, huh, Shanti?"

He pointed his finger at me. "Leece good man."

"Thanks. Shanti good man." I reached out, and we shook hands and smiled. We put our horses into a canter. It was a fine, clear spring day and they enjoyed the run. We stopped at a creek for water, and I handed

Shanti some jerky that Mr. Fitsimmons had given us. There were two cans of those peaches for supper.

We rode along and chewed awhile. Shanti said, "Leece woman go?" He kept looking straight ahead.

"Yeah. How did you know?"

Shanti said, "Bad," and patted his chest.

A few miles later Shanti reined in his horse and tilted his head back. He sniffed and pointed. "*Auna.*"

I couldn't smell anything. He said, "Cook fire no. Big fire yes."

"Let's go." I touched Packy with my heels and headed her for the cabin. After a minute I got my first smell of smoke. We came around the hill and caught sight of what used to be our home, a pile of ugly black cinders and ashes. A few lazy plumes of smoke ribboned up from the rubble. Our wood stove was all that was left standing. Shanti stopped at my side. "No-ear, bad man," he said.

The ground was still soft from the snow melt, and Shanti scouted around for tracks while I kicked through the ashes. There wasn't much to save. Dad and I had built the cabin with our own hands. Shanti rode over and got down beside me. He let me know that the horsemen had come from the southeast, burned the cabin, and ridden off to the northwest.

I asked, "How many?"

He drew in the ashes twelve lines and pointed to the northwest again. I figured they must have done this yesterday by the look of the cinders. Colby, Little Sam, and ten others.

I said, "Reece go." I pointed toward the tracks. "Shanti go home. Shanti *walama*. Reece kill bad man."

Shanti frowned at me. "Kill?"

I nodded and drew my Winchester from the scabbard. I pointed it and said, "Bang. Reece kill bad man. Shanti go home."

He motioned me toward my horse. "Leece, Shanti, kill bad man."

"No, this isn't your fight. Shanti go *walama*."

He slapped Asham on the rump and took off northwest. I followed him. The tracks were easy to trail, and we pushed the horses hard without talking until sundown.

We made a cold camp, wrapping ourselves in blankets and eating jerky and peaches. I was too worked up to feel like sleeping or talking, either one. The peaches didn't even taste good, but they went down easy. Shanti leaned back against a tree trunk eating quietly. A fire would have felt good, but it was too risky. It was going to be a long night of sitting and waiting for daylight.

We saw it together, the first hint of dawn. We gathered our gear and walked the horses northwest until there was enough light to ride by. Shanti led the way, and we began climbing the mountains around midday. I tried to ride without thinking too much. If I let myself think too much I would have used up all my anger. I wanted to save my mad for when we caught up with them.

Up ahead Shanti had stopped. He sat very still on Asham while I made my way up to his side. He just sat there with his head raised and eyes closed. After a minute he opened his eyes and turned to me. "Bad man go *walama*."

"Are you sure?"

He slapped Asham into a run, and Packy had a hard time keeping up. After an hour Shanti jumped off and ran alongside Asham for a mile or so. I jumped off Packy and tried to do some running of my own, but I didn't have the footwear for it, or the legs either. He had a pretty good lead by the time he swung back up on Asham.

We rode and ran into the afternoon. Shanti looked back now and then, and our eyes would meet for half a second. He was a good ways ahead, and I would lose sight of him from time to time, then catch another glimpse of his back when we rounded a turn or topped a hill.

I recalled the stream, the one that Big Nose had walked us through several days ago. Packy and I walked beside it up to the spring hole. Shanti had left Asham there and gone ahead afoot. I grabbed his reins, and we all three scrambled up to the top. I was heaving breath when I got a look down into the valley.

The next thing I did was vomit up those peaches.

✦ 32 ✦

Bodies were sprawled in the dirt. Shanti was bent over an unmoving form. He rose and ran to another figure laying facedown near the creek. I swung up into the saddle as Shanti ran to his lodge. We rode down into the valley. Packy tossed her head and skittished around as we made our way through the scattered corpses. The dead children bothered her the most.

The taste of peaches, foul and sour, stuck to the back of my nose. I stooped over and ducked inside the lodge. Shanti was squatting on the dirt floor, holding his mother's body and stroking her hair as he rocked back and forth. Toward the back wall were Big Nose's wife and baby lying in a heap.

I backed out of the doorway. Packy and Asham had trotted off down the valley, turning their backs on what I was looking at. None of the body shapes moved. There was no sound. I went into the next lodge and made myself feel each of the bodies, two women and two children, all were cold.

On my way to the next lodge I found Shanti's father with two bullet holes in his chest and an open slash across his neck. A rifle lay beside him. Flies buzzed his wound. I lifted the blanket from his shoulders and covered him. When I looked up, Shanti was standing with his mother in his arms. Her pretty black hair hung almost to the ground. He walked toward me and laid her at my feet. His face looked older. He pulled back the blanket and looked at his father. After a minute he let the blanket fall back over him. He looked up at me again and said, *"Saldu."*

I had nothing to say.

Shanti walked around the village and entered each lodge. He walked very stiff and straight. I recognized Skinny and Big Nose.

There was one soldier lying by the stream. He had sergeant stripes and an arrow through his back. I took his gun belt off, strapped it on, and pried the pistol from his fingers. He had a looking scope around his neck on a leather lanyard. I took that too.

Shanti was running across the creek to the house for the sick women. I checked the other bodies that lay on the ground in the fading light. When Shanti came out of the women's lodge, he wasn't straight and stiff anymore. He walked to me with his head down. As he passed, he whispered, "Mondala."

I said, "I'm sorry. I'm so sorry."

Shanti knelt between his mother and father and held each of their hands. He said some words, then joined their hands together and picked up the rifle. "Shanti kill white man."

I shook my head. "Me too. We'll do it together."

He looked at the sky. The first stars were appearing in the east. He pointed to the ground. "Reece fire."

I built a fire on the ground, ten feet away from the bodies. Shanti brought blankets and furs from his lodge and dropped them.

It was another sit-up night. Shanti began to sing quietly and rocked back and forth while the stars moved across the heavens. After a couple hours I found myself singing the song with him. It became a sort of chant that we kept up until first light, sending our sounds into the night.

At dawn Shanti held his father's rifle, an old Sharp's with a lot of rust. He carried a bow and quiver full of arrows too. As we trotted toward the horses, we cut across the trail of the raiders. Shanti looked at them and pointed west. *"Caverna,"* he said.

Packy and Asham were both nervous and contrary. After we left the valley, they settled down some. It was all like a bad dream, worse than any real dream I'd ever had, and there was no waking from it.

The riders we followed left clear sign heading for the cave of gold. I wondered how they knew the way. Who could have told them? I rode up abreast of Shanti and asked, "Map? *Map de la caverna de oro?* The cave of gold?"

He pointed behind us. *"Walama."*

"In your house. Your *casa? Walama* Shanti?"

Shanti slowed Asham and leaned sideways to study the trail sign. He pulled up and pointed to hoof prints. It took me a moment before I saw why he pointed. One of the horses was unshod, like the Yahi horses. Shanti slapped his horse into a run, and I chased after him wondering which one of his people could be riding with them.

An hour later Shanti left the trail and led us around a steep hill and through some pine woods. My stomach felt raw and empty. The headache was there, but only when I thought of it.

Shanti pulled up and jumped off his horse. He

pointed up the hill, and I followed him up the rise. The first hundred feet or so wasn't bad. After that it got steeper and slower going. I was mouth-breathing when we neared the top.

They were sixty yards away. There was open ground between us, and they were all facing the mountainside where the gold cave was. They were talking loud. I raised the scope and looked across.

I counted eight. Their camp was set up halfway between us in the clear ground. A fire was low burning under a coffeepot. The men were staggered up the mountainside. I saw Colby appear near the cave mouth holding a bag. He said something, and the men laughed as they passed the bag down the hill, first one, then another. The last man grabbed the sack and carried it to toward the fire. There were other bags there, four of them.

Shanti tugged my sleeve. He pointed off to the left. A man lay on his back, his face to the sun. When I trained the scope on him, I recognized the face. He wouldn't be jerking anymore. They hadn't needed the map after all. After he had led them to the cave, they must have killed him.

I passed the scope to Shanti. He started to look through the wrong end and I turned it around for him. I could hear the faint sounds of a hammer or pick.

It was an easy rifle shot, and the men clinging along the steep slope were without cover. I figured I could get at least five before they scrambled down. Colby first, I thought.

Sam must be in the cave with at least one other. There wasn't room for more than three. They'd be trapped in there and probably didn't have guns. We could wait them out and pick them off before they could make it down.

I laid the Winchester into my palm and looked down the sights at the back of a blue-shirted soldier. His suspenders made an X. I traced my way up the mountain, sighting each man in turn, each man's back.

I heard Shanti work the hammer of the Sharp's rifle. By the way he was holding it I knew he wouldn't hit anything. I reached across and pushed the gun down. He looked at me and frowned.

I motioned for him to follow me away from the hilltop, and scooted backward. I could still hear them laughing and shouting and wondered what kind of men they could be to be having a fun time after what they had done. What bothered me was shooting them like that without a chance. They needed killing, but there had to be another way. It might be days before the ones in the cave would risk coming out. Once it started, we would have to kill them all.

Shanti had crazy eyes. He kept his teeth together and said, "Shanti kill white man."

I nodded. "Later. We need to wait awhile and think it over."

"Shanti kill white man."

"Yeah, I know. Let me think a minute."

"Leece white man, no kill?"

"No, Shanti. Reece kill white man. Reece kill bad man."

Shanti started to scramble back up the hill, and I grabbed his ankle. He fought against me and kicked with his free leg, but I had better leverage and pulled him back down beside me.

He was plenty mad and struggled hard, but I held him fast. He didn't try to hurt me, he just tried to get loose. I pointed to my head. "Idea. Reece has idea. Listen." I motioned him farther down the hillside. I didn't have an idea, but went to thinking hard and came up with part of one. I began explaining it to him.

It took a long time. I had to point and use the words we both knew and draw pictures in the dirt. After a while he began to catch on. I went over it all once again, slower this time.

Shanti nodded. "Bad white man kill bad white man?"

"Yeah. That's the idea, Shanti."

"Hmm." He nodded one time, and we settled down to wait out the day.

◆33◆

They had settled into their blankets shortly after sundown. We waited for another three hours. The moon slipped in and out of the scattered clouds. We crawled to the hilltop and looked down.

Their fire had burned out. We could see the shapes of the men covered in blankets. Shanti looked at me, and I nodded. I took off the gun belt and holster and slipped the pistol down the back of my trousers. Shanti laid the rifle down, and we began crawling across open ground.

It was hard on the knees and elbows. We stayed side by side, stopping every few feet to look and listen. Someone was snoring, and when a spark popped from the fire, my heart stopped. Another man was snoring now, they sawed back and forth for a while until one of them mumbled and shifted under his cover. We flattened down and waited.

We were halfway there. I began moving again, and Shanti followed my lead. We stopped again, ten yards away. The pile of gold sacks was on the other side of the slumberers. I touched Shanti's arm and pointed to the right. He nodded and took a deep breath before crawling off.

We split up. I circled left, swinging wide of the men. Someone sniffed. Farther off to my left a horse whinnied. A thin cloud moved over the moon, and the light faded. I placed each elbow carefully, then a knee, then the other.

Shanti had made better time. I saw him reach out and take a sack from the top of the pile. I moved closer. It looked like there were eight sacks altogether. One of the sleepers grunted softly. I drew the revolver from my belt and waited. After a minute I returned the pistol and crawled the last few feet.

The sacks were heavier than I expected. I could only hold one in each hand and crawl. That meant two trips to get them all, and I didn't cherish that idea. Shanti must have felt the same way. He stood, hoisted two sacks in each hand and began walking around the far side of the sleepers. I picked up the other four bags.

The worst part was turning my back and walking over that open ground. I looked over my shoulder a couple times expecting to see one of them standing and aiming, but they slept right on through it. They were probably dreaming of being rich and living high with all their gold money. I followed Shanti back up to our lookout place. He dropped the gold sacks and did a little dance.

I let my sacks fall and did a dance with him, two boys dancing silently in the dark. For a half a minute I had forgotten what I had seen yesterday. Shanti remembered it, too, and stopped his dance at exactly the same time. He reached out, and we shook hands, then sat down to wait out the night. It was the third night without sleep for both of us.

We settled down to watch for sunrise. I lay on my side, Shanti leaned back against a boulder. There was some food in the saddlebags, but I didn't feel like going for it. I thought of many things, but the sight of Shanti's village kept returning. I turned on my back and watched the stars. There was a big red one that didn't blink and twinkle like the others.

I don't know when Shanti began crying. I just know that he had been at it for a while before I came aware. He was trying to be quiet and secret about it. I didn't move or let on, just lay there watching stars. I remembered how I had cried the day I buried Dad. There was no holding it back. Shanti had lost his entire family. His whole world was gone forever.

I walked over to him. He kept his head down, but I could see his shoulders shake. I sat down next to him and put my arm around his shoulder. He leaned against me, and we cried together.

ᐊ 34 ᐅ

Several men stirred under blankets in the early gray light, and the sound of muttered words reached us. I lowered the scope and looked over at Shanti. His eyes were red-rimmed and his lips were pulled back from his teeth.

One of the men slapped at the figure next to him with his hat. I heard, "Lemme alone," and raised the scope in time to watch them hat-womp each other, back and forth.

On the other side of the circle a man sat up and rubbed his eyes. He stood up and walked toward us, still wrapped in a blanket. After ten steps he parted the blanket and relieved himself. He buttoned up as he walked back and didn't notice that the sacks were gone.

He worked with the fire, added sticks from a pile, and poured water from a large canteen into a coffeepot. A pillar of smoke rose straight up in the still morning air. He placed the pot over the flames and took a drink from the canteen.

One of the hat slappers sat up and spoke. Through the scope I saw it was Little Sam. He leaned to the side and blew his nose with his fingers then wiped them off on the blanket of the sleeper next to him.

The sky was showing some blue in the east as the sun burned at the haze. Sam stood up, balled up his blanket, and dropped it. Another soldier rose and walked off to the left toward their tethered horses.

I counted eleven. There were two of us. I let my memory of Shanti's village go to work. Those men down there had killed women and children. They had probably taken pleasure from it. I was ready to get on with it.

The smell of coffee reached us. Coffee smells a lot better than it tastes, especially in the open. Even more when you don't have any of your own. Another figure sat up, then another. There were a lot of moans and yawns.

The first soldier took the pot off the flames, using his hat for a pot holder, and poured himself a cup. Little Sam and three others helped themselves. Through the scope I could see their faces wrinkle as they took their first sips. I could taste it. Colby was the last one to rise. He leaned up on an elbow and motioned to a soldier. The soldier handed Colby his cup. Colby took a swallow and handed it back, then got on his feet. He glanced at the ground behind him, where the gold sacks had been piled. I had been waiting for this time. Colby's shoulders stiffened. He pointed and said something to Little Sam.

Sam looked, then looked around, turning in a slow circle. Voices got louder. The men gathered to stand and stare at the ground where the sacks had been.

Two soldiers started pushing each other. Sam began throwing blankets around. I watched Colby through the scope as he counted the men, pointing out one at a time. When he was done, he counted again and frowned. Shanti was smiling. It wasn't a nice smile. The killing was about to start.

The two soldiers had quit shoving and gone to fist-fighting. The other men were shouting some foul talk and curse words. Sam called somebody "son of a bitch," and I jacked a shell into the Winchester.

Colby was kicking through the gear and opening saddlebags. The two fighting soldiers were rolling in the dirt, pulling hair, and digging at each other's eyes.

Sam had a pistol in his hand. He shoved it into the chest of the soldier who had started coffee. I saw the soldier shake his head. Sam swung the pistol, raking the soldier's face with the barrel sight. The soldier staggered back, then threw his coffee into Sam's face. Sam shot him twice in the chest.

The two soldiers stopped fighting at the sound of the shots, looked at each other, then went back to it again, even harder than ever. It must have been an old grudge.

Another man went to scrambling through his gear. He picked up a gun belt, drew the revolver, and Little Sam shot him in the back. He fell forward on his face, and Sam shot him again.

Everybody started grabbing for their weapons. Colby fired in the air and yelled, "Hold it, dammit. Everybody hold it."

The party froze. The two fighting soldiers were on their knees, gasping for air. "Put down your guns," Colby hollered. "We gotta figure this out."

There were nine to go.

The two fighting soldiers staggered to their feet and slapped at their clothes. The one on the left said something, and the other soldier spit at him. They spit back and forth a couple times, then went to wrestling in the dirt again. Colby and the others stood around and looked at the spot where the gold sacks had been. Several of them pointed. Little Sam said, "Somebody musta took them."

Colby looked at him. "That helps a lot, Sam."

Sam said, "Well, it weren't me."

The two soldiers had fought their way toward us. It was time to begin. I touched Shanti and made the motion of shooting a bow. I pointed at the two wrestlers, and he nodded.

A soldier spoke to Colby. "How many of us is there?"

"Eleven, everybody's here."

"How come who stole it didn't ride off?"

Colby said, "Go check the horses."

Sam said, "Maybe it's some kind of curse. You know, some kind of Indian curse."

Colby slapped him, backhanded.

Shanti raised up on one knee, drew his bow, and sent an arrow at the wrestlers. It caught the one on top in the neck, right below his hair line. The soldier grabbed at his throat, and the other soldier threw him off to the side and rolled on top of him. He hit him twice in the face before he noticed the arrow. He looked up toward us just as Shanti's second arrow whistled into the side of his chest, feather deep.

Seven.

I sighted in on Colby. The man who was arrow shot let out a yell. Everybody turned to look. A soldier moved into my line of fire, screening Colby. I center-shot him, worked the lever, and drew down on Colby. He was already running. I snapped off a shot that made him stagger and grab his leg. Before I could shoot again, he dove behind some boulders.

Sam was running the other way, to the left and toward the horses. He threw two shots over his shoulder as he ran. I led him, squeezed, and watched him spin as the bullet took him high in the arm.

The soldiers had gathered guns and were returning fire. A couple shots were close. I shot one in the hip. While I worked the lever, I saw an arrow take a soldier in the stomach. He dropped to his knees and held the shaft in both hands, staring down at it like he couldn't believe what had happened.

I glanced over toward Colby's rock, then turned to find little Sam. He was hidden behind a scrub cedar, and I put two quick shots through the branches.

Two soldiers were making for the horses, quartering away from us to the left. One lost his hat as he ran, and I saw his hair, done Indian style. The Sharp's boomed from beside me. I missed too.

Then the side of my face exploded.

I didn't pass out completely. I could hear gunshots on the other side of the high whistle scream from inside my head. I tried to get up, but everything was upside down and spinning.

"Leece. Leece."

I touched the side of my face, sticky and wet. Shanti was kneeling beside me. I pressed around some more. It felt pulpy, but my head was clearing. I crawled back up to the crest. The side of my face stung like a swarm of bees were at me.

A soldier tried to mount a bucking horse. He slid off, but kept a hold on the reins. I missed, levered a shell, and shot him in the back as he tried to climb back up again.

The horses ran off. There was one more soldier off to the left somewhere, the one who had Indian hair. Colby was wounded, behind some rocks to the right. Sam was shot, at least once and behind the scrub cedar.

My ear was ringing. I scooted down and began reloading. Shanti was standing, his bow in his hand, looking for a shot.

"Psst, Shanti." I motioned for him to get down. He took another look before he squatted beside me. I could tell by his look that my face must have looked pretty bad.

I pointed to the right. "One-Ear. Reece kill One-Ear. Shanti kill Yahi man." I pointed to the left where he was hidden.

Shanti took off his headband neckerchief and patted my face gently. I took the cloth from him and touched with my bare hand. I could feel little slivers of rock chips, stuck through the skin. I pointed again, "Shanti kill Yahi."

He shook his head no. "Shanti kill One-Ear bad man. Leece kill Yahi."

"No."

A voice came from below us. "Colby? Colby, I'm hurt bad, Colby."

I crawled back up the rise and looked down. Shanti was beside me. Sam spoke again. "Hey, Colby, did you get them?"

I turned to Shanti and whispered, "Shanti go, kill." I pointed off to the left. He looked into my eyes a moment, then nodded, backed down the hill, and moved off.

The rock I was behind had a long gouge where the bullet had hit. It was the shattered rock pieces that had hit my face. A lot of them were still in there.

Sam yelled, "Colby? Anybody? Jesus, I'm hurt real bad."

I said, "Come on out, Sam. Show yourself."

"Who is that?"

"Me, the curse."

"Where are you?"

"I come from the cave," I said, trying to make my voice sound deep and spooky. "I come from the cave and take back my gold while you sleep."

"Who are you?"

"The ghost of Wahemaloomawama," I said trying to make up a Yahi-sounding name. "The ghost who keeps the gold. Come out from behind that tree, or I'll shoot you."

"Does ghosts shoot guns?"

I shot the tree above Sam. "This one does." I fired again.

"All right, all right."

"Come out in the open."

"I can't. I'm shot. Got one in the shoulder, one in the ass."

"Here comes another."

"No, wait." Sam came crawling out from behind the tree. I reached for the scope and eyed him over. The butt shot had just grazed him, a long rip in the pants, oozing blood. He had the revolver stuck under his belt.

Blood dripped down my neck and under my collar.

Still nothing from Colby. The soldier who was gut shot from Shanti's arrow was moaning softly. He lay on his back and held the shaft with both hands. I said, "You can walk, Sam Aikens. Go see about your friend. Go see about Colby."

"Where is he?"

"To your left. Stand up and walk."

"I can't."

"Yeah, you can. If you don't, I'm going to shoot you in the other cheek."

He got up slowly, but he got up. "Now what?"

"Walk to your left. Your friend's behind those rocks."

Sam started moving. He was about thirty paces away from the rocks that Colby had ducked behind. I glanced to the left. Shanti had disappeared. Sam took another few steps. "I didn't know about the curse. Honest." He looked up toward me.

I hunkered down a bit. "Can you see Colby?"

"No."

"Keep walking."

He took a few more little steps and stopped. "Hey, I can see him. Hey, Colby?" He stood still a moment before he turned my way. "I think he's dead, Ghost. All I can see is his leg, but he ain't moving."

"Shoot him," I yelled. My face was swelling tight and pounding hard.

"Huh?"

"Shoot him. Shoot him in the leg."

"What for?"

"Because I got a rifle." I remembered, too late, saying those same words before.

Sam said, "Hey! That's you up there, ain't it, Reece?"

"Shoot him, Sam. Or I'll shoot you where you stand."

He touched his revolver, still searching for me with his eyes and inching closer to Colby's rocks. I said, "Do it now, Sam."

He gave it one more look and turned toward the rock, drawing his pistol. Just as it cleared his belt, a shot cracked from Colby's hiding place. Sam bent fast from the waist, staggered backward, and fell on his side. He kicked a minute, then lay still.

That left two.

I waited awhile, then worked my way along the hill-top, keeping the rocks in view. If Colby made a break, he would have to run twenty yards over clear ground before there was any cover. I got settled in, belly flat, my rifle in front of me, and waited. And waited. The sun climbed up to the hilltop across the way. I lowered my hat to shade my eyes. I wondered about Shanti and glanced that way now and then. Nothing moved.

An hour went by. I couldn't open my mouth at all. I thought of a lot of things to shout down at Colby but didn't say any of them. I remembered the picture in my head of him taking my shot, grabbing his leg, and scrambling on. It must have missed the bone.

The soldier who was gut shot let out another moan and lay back. His hands slipped from the arrow shaft and fell to his sides. Nine men were dead. I kept my lookout and picked slivers of rock from the side of my face. They were hard to get a hold of. One sliver had gone through my cheek. I could feel its sharp point with my tongue.

After another hour some buzzards showed up. *How do they know?* Was Colby watching them? Was he going to try to wait for dark? I thought about yelling to him, but held my silence. I knew where he was. He wasn't sure about me. I worked at another rock chip.

A movement caught my eye. I got a quick glimpse of the Yahi soldier moving between rocks. He was far off to the left, too far for a shot. I figured he had given Shanti the slip somehow and would make for the fort. He moved again, running between rocks and over the top of a far hill. I started to turn away, when Shanti emerged and trotted up the hill after the Indian soldier.

Silence from Colby's hideaway. There were five buzzards slow-circling overhead now. Their shadows swept the cleared ground. My right eye was closing.

⟐ 35 ⟐

Around noon Colby threw a rock from behind his boulders. It arced through the air and landed off to my left. *Now, what was that for?*

I worked at the rock sliver, trying to push it out with a thumb inside my cheek. It was wedged tight, and the side of my face was puffy and swollen, nearly closing my aiming eye.

Another rock looped up from Colby's hideaway. Getting restless, wondering if I was there, trying to draw me out. I thought about throwing rocks back. Bad idea. It was hard to think through the pain.

Two buzzards had landed and were picking at the bloody hole in the back of the soldier I had shot trying to climb on his horse. I turned and tried sighting in on them, holding the rifle left-handed, using my left eye to sight. My right eye kept trying to take over, and the sight picture jumped back and forth.

"Hey, Reece."

I shifted back around and stared at Colby's boulders.

"Come on, I know you're there. Let's talk."

The buzzards flopped and hopped at the sound of Colby's voice.

"Reece?"

A couple minutes dragged by. I listened to my breathing.

"Look, Reece. I can wait, longer you wait, the better for me."

Another two minutes.

"Soldiers are coming soon. Whole bunch of them. Let's talk now before they get here. They get here, you're done for. You know that?"

"Reece?"

I felt my right eye close shut. I could spread it open with my fingers, but it wouldn't stay.

"Let's you and me make a deal before they get here, while we still got the chance."

I scooted over to my right and used my knife to whittle off a branch from a bush.

"Soldiers will gun you down, Reece. That's fine with me. Thing is, they'll take the gold, and you or me neither one won't have none."

I figured about an inch and a half would do it. I cut off the branch and tried fitting it, one end shoving the eyebrow up, the other wedging the bottom eyelid down. I had to tilt my head back to aim down the sights.

"Here's what we can do, Reece. Split the gold up, you and me. Then you ride off. The soldiers get here, I'll tell them that some Injuns done it."

I cut off another stick.

"There's still plenty more gold in that cave. You and me the only ones know about it now. We'll divvy it up, fifty-fifty, and nobody'll know."

With two sticks the eye stayed open.

"Where's your horse?"

Now the trouble was my eyeball felt all dried out and I couldn't blink it.

"You by yourself, Reece? Listen, you got a partner, a three-way split is fine."

I stuck my little finger between the sticks and pulled my top eyelid down. It helped for about three seconds, then felt dry again.

"You get right down to it, one bag's aplenty for me. I'll take one bag, the rest is yours."

I pulled out the sticks and practiced aiming left-handed, left-eyed. I would just have to take my time.

"Is it a deal?"

The day was growing warmer. I slipped out of the parka and folded it up.

"Reece? How 'bout it."

The folded parka made a good gun rest. I got belly down and looked over the sights, pressed the parka flatter, and looked again. It was just about right.

"Okay, Reece. You don't wanna be rich, okay with me. We'll just wait, then, hear? Me, I'd rather be rich than dead. Don't say I didn't give you no chance."

The two buzzards had gotten used to Colby's talking and were back at it. A third one landed. What a lousy thing, being a buzzard.

After a few minutes Colby went to singing, letting me know what a good time he was having all hunkered down behind those boulders, shot in the leg. I counted off the days in my head. Kathryn would be leaving the day after tomorrow.

That was some girl, that Kathryn. I wondered if I would ever find me one as good. The thought of her leaving pulled an empty-feeling place into my chest. Maybe it wouldn't bother me all that much, knowing she used to be a whore.

Colby was doing, "Tum-tum-atum-tum-tum."

It would bother me some.

I spit in the dirt. There was some blood mixed in with it. Eight buzzards now. Three on the ground, five in the air. The sun felt good on my back. I swallowed some blood. It didn't make it all the way down and slickered my throat.

"I know you're up there, Reece. Say something."

A half hour later a buzzard swooped in next to Little Sam's body. It stood there, looking dumb. It ran its head under a wing and nosed around in there looking for something or other.

I could smell my own breath, sour and putrid. I bet buzzards have bad breath. And what do they talk about to each other? Guts?

Colby shot at the buzzard, and it jumped and flew away with big loud flops. The other buzzards flew off too. I wondered how many bullets he had.

It might be a mistake, letting Kathryn go. How does she know what I'd think about?

The buzzards came back after a while and brought back half a dozen of their pals and relatives. It looked like Colby was going to stick it out until dark.

I wondered about Shanti. His life had sure been pounded apart the last few weeks. A lot of it was my fault. If I hadn't made him come to town like that, maybe things would be different. Of course he would have been hanged if I hadn't ridden up when I had. Would he still want to live in his valley after all that had happened? Maybe he and I could both get a new start together somewhere else. Me and Shanti and Kathryn.

I wasn't paying attention when Colby reared up, took a quick look, then ducked back down. I didn't figure he spotted me in that quick, one-second look. I took a few deep breaths and started to yawn, but the right side of my jaw wouldn't give. I had to use my hand to push my mouth back shut. I pressed along the right side of my face. It felt like it was bulged out three or four inches now. Some water would be good. I glanced over at the canteens.

Colby peeked out again, too fast for me to get a shot off. Just a quick look before he ducked back down. Trying to draw fire, get an idea of where I might be. Not sure that I was there. Scared. Plenty scared now. The longer it went, the worse it would be for him.

I looked over my shoulder. Probably another three hours until sundown. If Shanti was with me I could send him around and let him come up behind Colby, lob a few arrows at him from the far hilltop.

Colby peeked up, ducked down, peeked up again, and yelled, "Reece," before he ducked back down. Nervous. Nervous and scared and shot in the leg. Probably pretty thirsty and hungry too. I found myself smiling.

Was I enjoying this?

I thought about it for a while. It had been exciting, pulling down on the men, rolling one after the other with snap shots. I didn't exactly enjoy it, but I didn't hate it, either, not the way I hated killing the animals. What did that mean? Later, when I had time, I would have to think about all that very carefully. Right now I had to kill Colby.

He spoke again, and this time I could hear the scare. "Look, Reece. It's gonna be dark soon, and I'll just sneak away and you won't know where I am or nothing. Best thing for both of us is you and me, we make our peace right now. See what I mean?

"Reece?"

I was propped up solid and sighted in on the last place he had raised his head. If he showed himself again, I would nail him for sure.

"Just each go our separate ways. You go your way, I'll go mine."

How long had we been like this? Eight hours, nine?

"Meet you in town, we'd pull a cork. We could be pals."

He peeked up again, but at a different place, along the left side of the rock. Before I could swing my rifle, he let off two quick shots at the place he had seen me last.

"Hey, Reece?"

Where would he show next time? Right, left, or center? I aimed at the right edge of the boulders and waited.

"Some of them ole boys you killed had wives, Reece. And little kids too."

My left eye was getting tired, doing the work for two. The swelling had spread to my nose. I could see a hump in it.

"You sure can shoot, Reece. Where'd you learn to shoot like that?"

He showed himself in the center of the boulders and threw a shot off to my right. I had guessed wrong. I stayed steady, holding a full bead on the right edge. Sooner or later . . .

"Hey, Reece, you know what? Little Sam, he told me that little whore wasn't no good at all. Said she was all wore out, been used so many times. That's what he said, Reece. Told me not to waste my time on her. Said she wasn't worth two cents, much less two dollars."

More buzzards were perched on top of the far hill. They looked like a row of men, dressed for a funeral in long black coats. Waiting.

"Nothing more useless than a wore-out skinny whore. She tried to get me to buy her lots of times. Everybody knows she's no damn good. Hear that?"

Colby chuckled to himself behind the boulders. His

words had got to me some even though I knew what he was up to. I took my finger off the trigger and wiped my hand along my pants. I squeezed my eye shut a few times and sighted back in.

His head came out just a bit lower than I was aimed at. The bullet took him high on the forehead.

He shouldn't have talked about Kathryn like that.

✦ 36 ✦

It took a while to get enough water, dribbling it in through my teeth. I built up the fire and put coffee water and beans to boil, then walked back around to Asham and Packy. Packy was nervous and worried about the way my face looked. I mounted up and rode her around the hill.

Asham followed along. I suspect he was worried about Shanti, and I was too. I palmed in some coffee grounds and stirred the beans. The buzzards watched from their hilltop perch. It was going to be a big job, getting all these men buried.

I felt around my jaw, pressing deeper with my fingertips through the swelling. Something was wrong in there. I held my bottom teeth and moved my jaw around. It sounded like a dog chewing chicken bones.

I sliced the jerky into small strips and added it to the boiling beans. The coffee was ready. I carried my cup with me as I strolled around and looked at the bodies, one at a time. There were ten of them. Most of the faces were young.

When I let myself think back on the battle, I could

feel the excitement all over again. Part of me had liked doing that killing. It was a part of me I had never known.

There was a big tin plate in the pile of gear around the fire site. When the beans were soft, I spooned them onto the plate and went to mashing them with a fork. After I added some more pot liquor and stirred things around into a soup, I started eating. It was slow going. I had to pry my teeth apart, slip in the spoon, then tilt my head back and let it slide.

The buzzards saw them first and flew off, gained some air, and circled way up high where the sun still shined. I watched the skyline and tilted back some more bean mash. They topped the rise off to the north, three of them at first, then another, then another until there were about twenty-five mounted riders looking down. Some of them wore head feathers.

I watched them, and they watched back. I mashed up some more beans and stirred them into the coffee. They began walking toward me on their horses, a steady stream of them coming over the rise behind the first bunch. It was hard to focus with one eye, but as they rode closer, I saw a hand raised to wave back and forth. Shanti. I waved back at him.

I dribbled in some more coffee and bean slush through my teeth while they came through the killing ground. Most of them had bows, a few had rifles, and the two up front carried long lances. They rode right up close and formed a circle around me. More riders topped the rise in the distance. No one spoke, not even Shanti.

After a while the one with the longest lance swung off his pony. He was dark-skinned with a wide mouth and broad forehead. He took his time looking things over before he walked over to me and looked down. I looked back up at him one-eyed.

He said, "You scared many warrior come?"

I nodded, "Yes, I'm scared."

"Why you not run?"

"Too tired. No sleep for three days, and my face hurts."

He thought about that. "Shanti Ma Teck say you give him life, say you friend to all my people. Say you speak truth, never lie. Say you good white man."

"No, I'm not all that good. Just Shanti's friend is all."

"Not friend to all my people?"

"I don't know all your people," I said. "Are you friends with all of them?"

He smiled slightly and shook his head. "Some Indian no damn good." He turned and said some words to his men. They began to drop from their horses. Shanti squatted beside me. He looked at my face and touched lightly with his fingertips.

"Bad," he said. He reached over and picked up a firewood stick. He held it in both hands and snapped it in two, then pointed at my jaw.

"Yeah, it's broke." I pointed to the pots. "Shanti eat beans, coffee."

He shook his head. His face looked worried. The braves were going through the equipment and saddle-bags. Shanti stood up and spoke to the head man, then brought him back to stand over me. A fresh scalp hung from Shanti's waist, and I didn't need to ask him if he had caught up with the Yahi in soldier clothes.

The man spoke in Mexican this time, "*Yo soy El Jefe Loco Caballo.*"

My mind was slowing down, and I wanted to sleep. It

208 ← Chap Reaver

took me a moment to figure it out. "The Chief Crazy
Horse?"

He nodded. "You hear my name?"

"No."

"You hear name Sitting Bull?"

"No."

"You hear name General Crook?"

"No."

"General Sheridan?"

"No."

"General Custer?"

"No."

"General Sherman?"

"No. I don't get around much."

The braves were picking up the rifles and sticking
revolvers under their clothes. I picked up my rifle and
held it across my lap.

Crazy Horse said, "We fight now, all the general
man, all the soldier. You fight with my people? You fight
with soldier?"

I looked around at the dead bodies. "I am tired, Mr.
Crazy Horse. I sleep now, and when I wake up I will
fight no more, ever." I handed him my rifle and leaned
sideways to drag two blankets toward me.

Crazy Horse said, "All men fight."

I laid on my left side and closed my eye. "This one
doesn't, not anymore. I've had enough." Shanti arranged
the blanket over me as I drifted off. For the first time, I
felt like a man.

In the middle of the night I came awake. Shanti was
squatted beside me, his hands resting softly on my jaw
and cheek. I said, "Shanti."

He said, "Leece, bed."

I reached out and touched his arm. "Reece and

Shanti go together. Build house, *wowi*. Much gold for land."

He pulled my hand from his arm. "Shanti kill white man."

-37-

In the morning Shanti fixed me tea and cut some hollow-center sticks to suck it through. There must have been two hundred warriors in sight, maybe more. Smoke from cook fires mixed and blended under a dark-clouded sky.

The side of my face pounded with each step I took away from the camp, but wasn't too bad if I moved slow. I walked behind a cedar tree and relieved myself. As I came back toward our fire, I saw the bodies of the soldiers heaped into a tangled pile.

Shanti was talking with Crazy Horse. I helped myself to some yuna and added some water so that I could suck it through the hollow stick. One splinter of rock was still stuck through to the inside of my cheek and scraped against a tooth.

Crazy Horse turned to me. "We go, you stay."

I sucked and nodded.

"No more stay on reservation. No more sign treaty with general. General not make treaty promise to keep."

I looked at my best friend. "Shanti go?"

He shook his head yes.

"Don't forget your gold." I pointed over my shoulder. *"Oro amarillo."*

Crazy Horse said, "Gold no good for the people. We fight soldier with Sioux, Cheyenne, Dakotas—all fight as one. Make soldier run from hunting lands."

I said, "You kill one soldier, two more soldier come. Kill two and four more come. Many will die, Crazy Horse."

"To die in battle is good. To live in reservation like cows is slow death. Soon all dead warriors will return to drive white man from our land."

"Return from where?"

"From world of spirits."

"Where'd you get that idea?"

"It is true. Sitting Bull dream with ghosts. Spirits speak with Sitting Bull. The ghosts of all dead warriors ready to come. Send white man from our land forever."

"I don't think so, Crazy Horse. Ghosts like it real well where they are now. I wouldn't be counting too much on them coming back if I was you."

"Sitting Bull dreams the truth. Spirits come in his dreams."

It was easier to speak if I pushed under my chin with one hand and spread my lips with the other. "I had a dream like that once. I spoke with my father, my grandmother, and brother. Some other people who were dead. It seemed very real, as real as being here with you. But I don't know, maybe Sitting Bull's dream didn't mean what he thought it did."

"Sitting Bull dreams with ghosts. The ghosts tell him they return soon, send white man away from this land."

"Maybe Sitting Bull is lying."

"I believe in the dream of Sitting Bull."

"I've never heard of a ghost coming back from the dead. I've heard a lot of men tell lies, though."

"Sitting Bull does not lie."

"Maybe he had a dream, maybe he believed it. That doesn't mean you should believe it."

Crazy Horse looked at me and smiled like he felt sorry for me, being so dumb. I said, "I used to have scary dreams when I was a little kid. Fever dreams with monsters and skeletons. They seemed real too. Then I almost died and had a wonderful dream, like in heaven. It seemed real, too, but it might have just been the other kind of dream, upside down. See what I mean, Crazy Horse? If you can't believe your own dreams, not all the way, you sure shouldn't feel obliged to believe some other man's."

"Sitting Bull dreams the truth. That is what I know."

I started to argue with his words, but stopped. I wasn't going to change his mind, so I sucked up some more yuna.

Shanti said, "Leece go Macland?"

I shrugged, then nodded. Crazy Horse spoke to a young man with his chest all painted up. The warrior walked away and began shouting to the others. Shanti touched my arm. He pointed off, and we began walking.

Our horses were standing side by side. My face must have looked pretty bad judging from the way Packy bulged her eyes and worried at it. After she nuzzled it and I told her I was all right, she felt better.

Shanti said, "Leece, Shanti kill bad man."

I nodded. He said, "Leece, Shanti, Fismon man, Fismon woman."

I said, "Reece, Shanti go *wowi.*"

He said, "Leece, Shanti," and made laughing sounds.

I said, "Reece, Shanti," and made crying sounds.

The braves had mounted their ponies and horses and were straggling by, moving south. Shanti held my hand, and we shook for a long time, looking into each other's faces, getting them set in our memories.

When the last of the warriors passed, Shanti put his arms around me. We embraced for a few seconds, patting each other's shoulders and backs.

Shanti turned away quickly and swung up on Asham and looked down at me. He worked with his mouth, shaping his lips carefully before he said, "Arreece."

His first *r* sound. I smiled at his back as he started off, then remembered and shouted, "Shanti, wait."

He turned in the saddle, and I walked over to him and handed him the blue neckerchief. It was stiff with my dried blood. He took it and nodded one more time before he reined Asham around and slapped him into a run. I watched his back until he was out of sight. He never looked back.

The soil was shallow, an inch or two of dirt over hard pan rock. I scratched around several places with a shovel and tried to figure out some way to cover the bodies. There was no way. The buzzards would be fat.

I put together a bedroll and gathered some cooking gear from the supplies scattered around. Packy followed me and tossed her head. I was anxious to leave too.

A slow drizzle began as I climbed onto the saddle. It came certainly, settling in for the day. We put our backs to the killing ground and moved south. We hadn't traveled long when I remembered the gold. Packy argued about turning back.

I hid seven bags inside a rock pile and stuffed one inside my bedroll, then retied it. When I got back on the saddle, Packy laid her ears back and broke into a steady gallop. A few minutes later I turned for one last look and saw the buzzards, circling low under the gunmetal skies.

I had to hold my jaw with one hand until I got Packy slowed down into a walk that didn't jounce so hard. She tried to put her hooves down easier. I slipped off my belt and cinched it around my head and under my chin. It helped a little bit.

The drizzle kept us company through the day, softening the light and the sounds. We were the only thing moving through the hills. As darkness began, I thought about making camp, building a fire. I wasn't hungry, and a night in wet blankets and clothes didn't promise comfort.

It was hard to talk through clenched teeth with a swollen tongue and puffed-up jaw. "Feel like going all night?" I asked.

✦38✦

We turned heads, Packy and me, when we dragged into Macland the next afternoon. People watched from the boardwalk and stared out shop windows. Packy slogged through the mud, one step at a time, the same pace she had held for the last twenty hours or so.

It was warm and dry in Fitsimmons's stable. Packy went to work on a bucket of oats while I wiped her down and sweet-talked her. By the way she chewed I could tell that she was tired too.

My boots squished, and my pants were waterlogged and heavy. I had to hold them up as I crossed the street to the hotel. The clerk was reading a newspaper behind the counter.

I spoke through clenched teeth. "Give a room."

"What happened your face?"

"Got shot. I want a room."

"Jesus Christ," he stood behind the counter and leaned toward me for a closer look. "Holy Mother."

I handed him a gold chunk. "Put my saddlebags in the safe. I want a room, a bath, some soup, some dry clothes."

"This here's gold," he said.

"I know. I want you to tend to me."

"I will. Yes, sir. Anything you want." He turned and worked the dial of a floor safe. He swung the door open, and I handed him the saddlebag. He tested the weight in his hand. "Is that gold in there?"

"Yeah."

"Son of a bitch. Must be twenty pounds, twenty-five. Goddamn son of a bitch."

"Put it away and don't cuss."

"Yes, sir. I won't say nothing bad no more neither." He slammed the door and spun the dial. "You church people?"

"A room," I said.

"Yes, sir. How about number one? That's our best." I nodded.

He reached for a key and came around the counter. "I'll show you right on up."

"I can find it. Go turn that into cash. Send me up some soup, lots of soup. Some hot water for a bath."

"How about a steak? You look like you could use a big steak, maybe some eggs, fried potatoes."

I could taste the steak. "Just soup."

"Soup, right. Whole lot of soup. I'll be right with you."

He was back with a big quart jar of chicken soup before I got undressed. "Boy's bringing up some water, Mr. Reece. Be right up. And here's your change. Hunnert forty-four dollars, eighty cents."

"For that one piece of gold?"

"Yes, sir. You're rich, ain't you, from the feel of them saddlebags? I took out for the room and soup."

I sucked up some soup through the hollow stick Shanti had given me. Different parts of my body perked up and asked for more. It hurt me to leave the bits of chicken in the bottom, but I knew I couldn't get them past my teeth.

"I ain't never seen a feller eat like that, sir, Mr. Reece."

I handed him the jar. "The stage get in yet?"

"Yes, sir, Mr. Reece. Got in, oh, two, three hours ago. Sure did. Couple passengers staying here for the night."

"So it hasn't left yet?"

"No, sir, Mr. Reece. Road is pretty bad with all the rain. Gonna leave tomorrow morning, the weather clears."

A youngster came in with two buckets of steaming water. He set them by the washbasin and tried not to look at my face. He was about ten years old and real skinny.

I asked the clerk, "What's your salary?"

"What, sir?"

"How much money do you make?"

"Three dollars, sir. Three dollars a week, and I get my room."

"Here's twenty dollars. Get me more soup, just the juice part."

"It's called the broth, sir."

"Yeah, just the broth. Two quarts. Keep the change."

"All of it?"

"Yeah, get going." I turned to the boy. "What do they pay you?"

He shrugged his shoulders. "Nothing."

"What do you mean, nothing?"

"They let me stay here and eat."

"Where's your ma and pa?"

"Dead, Ma is. Pa, he just up and gone somewhere."

"What's your name?"

"John Barry."

"Okay, John Barry. Would you go over to Fitsimmons's store? Tell him Reece needs some clothes. Everything except boots and belt." I handed him twenty dollars. "Shouldn't be more than three or four dollars."

He nodded.

I said, "Who looks after you?"

"I don't need anybody. I can take care of myself."

"You got any brothers or sisters?"

He shook his head.

"You all by yourself?"

He shrugged his shoulders.

"Well, I'm by myself and I'm ugly, but could you look after me for a while? I'm not as tough as you are."

"Sure."

"Go get me some clothes."

I didn't know who that was looking back at me in the wash mirror. The right side of his face looked like a half a melon with a thick, crusty scab over it. The skin around the scab was a deep purple-blue. When I took off the belt, it left a sunk-in place. I poured some hot water in the basin and got started. I did my face and hair first and worked my way down, poured the soapy water back into the bucket and did everything again with fresh water.

I heard the clerk hit the steps on the run and wrapped a towel around my middle before he came in.

He grinned real big. "Got you a quart of beef broth, quart of chicken. Nice and hot."

I sat on the bed and went to sucking. He said, "What else you want, sir, Mr. Reece?"

"Just stay around, don't talk."

"Yes, sir."

John Barry came in with Mr. Fitsimmons and an

armload of clothes. Mr. Fitsimmons frowned up his face at the sight of mine. I said, "I'm okay."

"What happened, Reece?"

"Colby shot at me," I said. "Hit a rock near my head, and the pieces of rock whopped me up side of my face. My jaw bone's broke."

John Barry laid new clothes on the bed and handed me some coins.

Mr. Fitsimmons said, "Where's Colby?"

"Dead." I took the ten-dollar gold piece, put it in John Barry's hand, and closed his fingers over it. "Sam's dead too. Whole bunch of guys are dead."

"What you gonna do?"

"Give some sleeping lessons soon as I finish this soup." I looked at the clerk. "It's been three, four days since I've slept. You make sure you wake me before the stage leaves, hear?"

The clerk said, "Yes, sir. Mr. Reece. And I'll see nobody disturbs you. Stay right outside your door."

Mr. Fitsimmons said, "What are you going to do about your face?"

"Eat soup and hope it heals up."

"How about Shanti?"

"He's . . . I'll tell you everything later. Right now I need to sleep."

They filed out the door, and I climbed under the covers. Maybe when I woke up, my face and jaw wouldn't hurt so bad. The door opened, and John Barry looked in, just his head stuck through the door. I looked back at him. We stayed like that for a minute, then he started to back out.

I said, "Hey."

His head peeked around again.

"You want to stay in here?"

He shrugged his shoulders.

"If you want to, it's okay."

"You want me to?"

"Yeah, I'd like that."

"Well, okay. If that's what you want."

"That's what I want."

"Don't do it 'cause you're sorry for me."

"I'm not sorry for you."

"I don't like it when people feel sorry for me."

"Me neither, so shut up and let me sleep."

◆ 39 ◆

My bladder pressed me out of a deep sleep, and I found the bed pan without waking all the way. John Barry was laying on the floor, scrooched up on his side with his hands under his head. I carried him over to the bed. He whimpered a little bit as I laid him down. I scooted in aside him and got us covered. He was about the age my brother would have been if he had lived.

I piled up some more sleep before hands shook my shoulder. "Mister, hey, Mister?"

I opened my eye.

John Barry said, "The stage," and pointed to the window.

I jumped up and looked out. The stage was just rounding the last of the shops.

"Dang!" I went through the clothes and started dressing.

John Barry rubbed his face. "I'm sorry, Mister."

"It's all right. It wasn't your job."

"You ain't mad?"

"No, just in a hurry." I buttoned my shirt.

He sat my boots by the chair. "Did you put me in your bed?"

"Uh-huh."

"Your face looks awful."

"Yeah, I know."

"I never saw a scab that big before."

I pulled on a boot. "It's a beauty, isn't it? What do you figure that scab would weigh? Three, four pounds?"

"Why'd you put me in your bed?"

"Well, I didn't want to trip over you." The boots were still damp.

"I like to sleep on the floor."

"Stop it, John Barry. Just stop it. I'll be your friend if you let up a little." The parka was damp, too, but I shrugged it on and started for the door. "See you later, pal."

"We're not really pals."

"Yeah, we are."

"You coming back?"

"Yes."

"Promise?"

"Yep."

"That's what my dad said, and he never come back."

"Well, I'm not your dad."

Me and Packy dug out after the stagecoach, throwing mud. Sleep hadn't helped the jaw any, and I held the reins with one hand, my face with the other. After a half hour we pulled the stage in sight.

The rain had stopped, but the clouds were solid and gray. I rode behind the stage and tried to think of some good words. After a few minutes of that I gave up and gave Packy the go-ahead. We galloped up alongside and caught sight of Kathryn, all fitted out with a hat and everything. She looked surprised.

I waved at the driver until he braked down his team. "What do you want?"

I pointed at the coach. "I gotta talk to somebody in there."

"What's a matter with your head?"

I slid off Packy and opened the coach door. There was a man beside Kathryn in gentleman's clothes, a man and woman on the other seat. I said, "Hello, Kathryn."

"What are you doing here, Reece? What happened to you?"

"Look, I don't want you to go. I mean, to Saint Louis."

Kathryn looked at the other passengers. "I've already paid, Reece. And I already told you about everything."

"Yeah, but, what I mean is, I've thought about it some. I've changed my thinking on some things."

"Well, I haven't. Reece, your face looks like it's going to bust."

The passengers were turning their heads as we talked, first to me, then back to Kathryn. I said, "Could you come out here?"

"No."

"Come on."

The driver leaned around. "I'm half a day behind, fella."

The man next to Kathryn pulled out his watch. I said, "I just want to talk a minute, ask you something."

"Ask me what?"

The passengers faced my way. I said, "It's real private."

They looked at Kathryn. She said, "We've done that, Reece. We've had our private talk and got things settled."

"There's something else I've got to say."

"What?"

Four faces looked at me. I said, "I killed a bunch of

men, Kathryn. I killed Colby, and Sam Aikens, and some
soldiers I didn't even know. Me and Shanti, we gunned
them down."

"What's that have to do with me?"

"I want to talk to you about it."

"Why?"

"Because. Because I liked it, and I didn't like it that I
liked it. I've decided that I'm never going to kill again.
I've made up my mind."

"So?"

"So, I mean, do you believe me?"

"Yes, I believe you."

"Well, Kathryn. I believe you, too, don't you see?
I'm not going to kill anymore and you're not going to
. . . you know. It's all behind us, both of us, and we
don't have to talk about it or think about it. We can just
start from right where we're at right now."

She turned and looked out the far window.

I said, "Could you still like me some, Kathryn,
knowing I was a killer for a time?"

She kept her head turned.

"Well, I sure do like you, Kathryn."

We all looked at the back of her head. The lady in
the other seat leaned toward me and whispered, "Tell
her you love her."

It wasn't as hard to say that as I thought it would be.
"I love you, Kathryn."

I watched the back of her head some more. We all
did. The lady looked at me and nodded, so I tried it
again, "I love you, Kathryn."

She kept her head turned. I said, "We found the gold
cave. I've got a whole lot of money now, more gold than
I can carry."

Kathryn was smiling when she faced around. She

tilted her head to the side real cute and said, "I love you, too, Reece."

I said, "How about coming back with me?"

"You sure?"

"Yes."

"I guess you need someone to look after you, huh?"

"Yeah, I need you."

"Really?"

"Yes. And you need me too."

She leaned forward, smiled an "Excuse me" to the passengers, and came into my arms, just the right size.

➤ 40 ➤

June 1906

A young Indian boy pointed the way for me, and I rode Packy through the reservation, trailing Asham on a short lead. Shanti was sitting on a wooden bench outside the government reservation store. He wore a blue neckerchief like a headband. It still looked good on him.

He recognized Asham first, rose from the bench, and squinted his eyes as we rode close. "Reece?"

"Hello, Shanti."

His smile was exactly the same. I sat my saddle and watched him stand to look Asham over and pat his rump. "Grandson?" he asked.

"Great-grandson," I said. "Climb on."

He swung up, not as lightly as he had thirty years ago. Asham spread his eyes and pranced back a bit. Shanti stroked his neck and spoke in low tones. I touched Packy with my heels. Shanti got Asham settled and rode up beside me. "Why do you come, Reece?"

"Collecting rent," I said.

"Rent?"

"Uh-huh. The thirty dollars you owe me."

"Why do I owe you this dollars?"

"For the valley. Your old home place, *wallama*. I bought it with the gold money, and I've been renting it to you. I read about you in the newspapers, finally surrendering. So, I thought I'd come see you. Get you to pay up."

Shanti kicked Asham into a canter and yelled back over his shoulder, "Race you for it, Reece."

We sprinted away from the settlement, through the open plain. Asham had more leg than Packy, and I wasn't all that keen on racing anyway. After a minute Shanti slowed and let us catch up. "A fine horse," he said.

"It's yours."

"This is not my horse."

"Yeah, it is."

"It is not my horse, Reece."

"It is if I say so. Don't argue about it, Shanti. It gives me pleasure to give it to you. Let me have a pleasure."

"I cannot."

"I rode nine hundred miles to give you that horse, Shanti. Now, take it, or I'll have to drag you off him and beat the snot out of you."

Shanti smiled. "I am tired of fighting, Reece. I will take this fine horse."

We stood our mounts and looked back while they blew and grazed on clover grass. We had outrun the flies, and a breeze carried a sweet smell.

Shanti said, "I think of you many times."

"Me too."

"I fight side by side with many men, Reece. I ride many miles with others. I sit around many fires and talk of many things. When I think 'friend,' I always think Reece."

"Yeah, I'm sort of the same way."

"Our time was good, you and me."

"Yes, it was, Shanti." We looked at each other. I said, "Would you like to go home?"

"Home?"

"Yeah, *wallama*. Want to see it again?"

He looked away. "I stay here, Reece. I sign papers with general to stay here and make no more war."

"Well, I signed papers, Shanti. The papers say that you have a pardon and are free to go where you want to go."

"This is true?"

"It is true."

"We leave soon?"

"I'm ready whenever you say."

"Then we go now. This place smell like shit."

There is deep pleasure in riding a good horse on a long trail and getting to know someone with easy conversation. We let the horses and the talk find an easy pace.

I did most of the talking the first day, telling Shanti about my life with Kathryn, John Barry, our three daughters, our grapes and apples.

We stayed clear of towns and camped beside free streams. Shanti told me about Bull Run, his running war with the soldiers over five states and twenty-nine years. He showed me the scars from many wounds.

I said, "The ghosts never came, did they?"

He sighed, and shook his head. "No, just soldiers. More soldiers and more soldiers, bigger guns."

I showed him the arrowhead, worn smooth from the years against my chest. He rubbed it with his thumb. "Flint get smooth, skin get rough." He touched the side of my jaw, pressing his fingers along the old break. "This from Colby?"

"Yeah. Kathryn says I'm more handsome this way."

He shook his head. "Ugly. Does your face scare little children and make them cry?"

"Sometimes."

"Did you swing the arrowhead to find me?"

"No, I had a map, and a compass."

"The arrowhead no longer swings?"

"I don't know, Shanti. I didn't try it. I knew the map would get me there."

"Not sure with arrowhead, huh, Reece?"

"That might have just been luck."

"Do you talk with hawks, Reece? Speak to trees?"

"No."

"Dream with ghosts?"

"No."

"All white man now."

"I guess so, Shanti."

He nodded. "It is good. I am Yahi forever."

We stopped at a creek and watered our horses. Shanti laid flat on his belly to drink. He would take a long pull, then look up before drinking again, the way deer do it. I rinsed my canteen and drank from the spout.

On the sixth day we rode up the stream, past the spring pool, and scrambled up the hill to look out over the hidden valley. We were both breathing heavy as we looked down. Either the hill had gotten steeper or we had become older. There was no sign left of the old village.

Shanti said, "The memory of home is in the blood of the salmon. I would want my bones to lie here with the sacred bones of my people."

"You can live here if you want," I said. "I deeded it over to you. Papers are in Macland, at the courthouse. There's money in the bank for you."

"This land is mine?"

"Yeah, it always has been."

"I can live my days here?"

"Yeah."

"You live here, too, Reece?"

"No, I've got my own home to go to back in California. Two grandsons to watch grow. Another grandchild on the way. You could come back with me if you want. You'd be welcome there."

He looked out with his fine, dark eyes, then turned in the saddle and offered his hand. "I stay."

I nodded. He squeezed my hand hard before letting go, then touched Asham with his palm and rode down the hill. I knew he wouldn't look back.

About the Author

Herbert Reaver, known to his friends as Chap, is a chiropractor who lives and practices in Marietta, Georgia. He and his wife, Dixie, have been married for over thirty years and have two grown sons, whom Dr. Reaver numbers among his best friends. His avocation is racquet sports. His addiction is writing.

Chap Reaver's writing has appeared in several humor and professional publications. His first novel for Delacorte Press, *Mote*, won the 1991 Edgar Award from the Mystery Writers of America for Best Young Adult Novel.